THE ENCHANTED ORCHARD

SUMMER OF 1980

THE ENCHANTED ORCHARD

SUMMER OF 1980

Rob Boss

WWW.JESOCIETY.ORG

Paperback Edition July 30, 2023
ISBN 978-1-7379026-8-3
© 2023 Rob Boss

A publication of JESociety Press
Visit www.jesociety.org

ImagesofDivineThings.com

For permission requests and inquiries,
Email: rob@jesociety.org
Web: www.jesociety.org

Cover art: *Flowering Orchard* (Vincent van Gogh, 1888).

Contents

THE MOVE

OUR CAR IS CRAMMED TO THE BRIM with suitcases and duffel bags, and when we ran out of luggage, we used black trash bags. I feel that we look like the Beverly Hillbillies, but it's an adventure! The sights and sounds of country roads, cows mooing, horses galloping, shade trees with swings, little churches, convenience stores, people mowing their lawns, and everything else that is part of small-town rural life fill me with happiness and good memories as we drive out of town.

Mom slows down as we reach an intersection. I look around once she comes to a stop to see why she stopped here. Normally, I would see folks selling tomatoes, watermelons, or any other type of produce from their garden on the side of the road, but this is different. There are no vegetables or fruits, only puppies.

"David, I'm going to give you something you've never had before - your own dog," Mom says to me. "I'm so proud of how you're handling this move and all of the other changes in our lives."

I can hardly restrain myself.

"Are you serious, Mom? I've always wanted a dog! I promise I'll take care of it!!"

I've always questioned why I didn't have a dog. Maybe I wasn't responsible enough, or maybe there were rules where we lived that prohibited us from having a pet.

Things have changed since then. We're relocating to the country, and I'll be able to have a dog. As we get out of the car and look at the animals, my attention is pulled to a small black and white spotted bird dog puppy.

"Take your pick," the man calls out, "they are all fine dogs!"

I point to my choice and name him Spotty. He is the most wiggly little dog. When he eats, he shivers with excitement. My puppy will be my best friend. I dream of all the things Spotty and I will do when we move into that wonderful place - Grandma and Granddad's house.

We're driving down the road, Spotty is squirming in my lap, and memories are filling my thoughts. It's always a thrill to visit my grandparents in rural North Central Texas, but now we get to live there!

————

Spotty and I are now living in the happiest of places, full of great memories. Spotty, however, has to be an outside dog because my grandparents don't allow pets in the house.

We awoke early one morning, not long after arriving at my grandparents' place, to loud snarling, yelping, and squealing.

Granddad looks outside before running to retrieve his rifle. I witness a horrific sight through the screen door.

"SPOTTY!!!!!" I yell.

Spotty is being killed by coyotes on the front porch. It is too late for Granddad to intervene; they are dragging Spotty across the field. Granddad shoots a few shots at the coyotes, but they miss. Spotty was gone and I am devastated. I've been in a depression for several days. No amount of happy memories can compensate for Spotty's death, and everything appears to go downhill from there.

————

I quickly realize that there is a difference between visiting grandparents and living with them. It's simply different and occasionally unpleasant. My parents split earlier this summer of 1980. I am 12 years old and have no idea why this happened, believing it was my fault. I'm not sure why it happened so suddenly, yet it seemed to have been a long time coming. So here I am, without my dad, without knowing where he has gone.

My mom has returned to college to complete her degree, and she is struggling to afford rent and tuition payments. Life is difficult, and despite her efforts to hide me from it, it has reached the point where both rent and tuition cannot be paid.

"Son, you know how hard things have been. I simply cannot do everything that has to be done. We need help if we are to survive this time of our lives. I'm sad that your dad isn't here. I can't explain everything right now, but perhaps later. We'll have to move in with Grandma and Granddad."

I recall her being extremely unhappy when she told me about the upcoming move. I don't feel sad, but rather delighted.

"You look depressed, Mom. But this could be fantastic!"

I'm not sure if she asked to move back in with her parents or if they offered her assistance, but I know it's humiliating for her. Everyone desires their own home, to be in control, and to be considered an adult. My mom returns to her childhood bedroom, which still has the same furnishings and decorations. It's very difficult. She begins to suffer from depression.

I overhear her sobbing and lamenting to herself, "I feel like my life has taken a two-decade step backwards!"

To make matters worse, several members of Grandma and Granddad's church avoid my mom due to her divorce.

"Did you hear about the preacher's daughter?"

"No surprise there. I knew it wouldn't last. That apple fell pretty far from the tree. Kids today know nothing of commitment or sacrifice."

She wonders if she will ever find love again or if things will ever improve. She struggles to believe in God because she feels abandoned and alone.

———

Moving in with my grandparents requires downsizing. This surprised me. I'm not sure where our furniture went, and I'm not sure where a lot of my personal belongings disappeared to. They have vanished in the move, and we have all suffered as a result.

"Mom, where is my little camera and my box of books?"

"Please stop asking, David! It will all get sorted out soon."

I'm not conscious of how quickly my life is changing. I know I'm in a new place for the long haul, but I also know it's Grandma and Granddad's house. Now that I live there, I am separated from my closest friends. I live under my grandparents' roof and have to conform to their rules and routines. I don't have a room; the living room serves as my bedroom. Even though I have the swamp cooler, which I like, and all of my other memories, yet everything is different now. The home has lost some of its luster in various ways.

As a 12-year-old boy, some of the most important things I miss are my room and my makeshift desk, which was a large square chest on which I kept books and a lamp. I miss my encyclopedias; I had two sets, a regular A-to-Z encyclopedia and a 26-volume animal encyclopedia.

I long for the ocean. As a kid, I am tired of the country's dry, dusty roads and the city's heated concrete. I collected seashells, dried starfish, dried pipefish, and dried seahorses, which I kept on my desk next to my books.

I miss my aquarium, where I had goldfish and other aquatic critters. One time I sent off for sea monkeys after seeing them advertised in the back of a magazine. They didn't survive long and didn't resemble the images in the advertisements.

I also ordered seahorses one time. To my surprise, they arrived in a small bag of water, and the seahorses were alive and swimming around. That was a cool moment. In my excitement, I filled the tank with freshwater, but unfortunately I did not prepare the water properly and introduced the seahorses too early. They perished instantly.

Now there is no aquarium, desk, encyclopedias, sea monkeys, seahorses, or goldfish in my life, and they are unlikely to reappear anytime soon. There is no room, no belongings, and no privacy.

"Are we living closer to the ocean now? Can we go to the beach soon? Dad said he would take me!"

"Sorry David, we moved north. The beach is south. We will take a trip there as soon as we can."

I let out a long sigh.

My bed is the couch in the living room. In terms of comfort, it's okay, but there is no privacy. There is no way out, nowhere I can go to be alone. Sleeping in the living room is challenging because I can only go to bed after everyone else has. There is no bugging out as long as grownups are present and talking into the evening. And there are nighttime disturbances.

Granddad is of the age when he needs to use the restroom two or three times during the night. On his way to the restroom, he passes straight past the couch where I'm sleeping. I am frequently jolted awake by his shuffling or the flushing of the toilet.

"I'm sorry, go back to sleep," he says quietly.

I know he tries to be quiet; I know I should be more patient and grateful. But I'm a self-centered kid, and nothing is right if my world isn't right. Granddad is an early riser; he wakes up at 5 a.m. every day. I'm bothered once again.

COUNTRY LIFE

L IFE IN THE COUNTRY may not have everything, but it does have things that you won't find in the city: swimming holes, catfish, bullfrogs, bobcats, turkeys, and bugs—way too many bugs! My grandparents are country people who like everything about country life; they prefer sandburs over sirens any day.

———

Grandma and Granddad live in a modest house that was most likely built in the 1930s or 1940s. The screened-in porch and rocking chairs are prominent aspects of the home. I enjoy sitting and rocking in those chairs, especially in the summer evenings when the fireflies are putting on their own fireworks display. And I love those fireworks, where we can see the bugs fly around and blink their lights.

"Davy boy, pull your chair over here. Let's watch some fireworks!"

"It's not the 4th of July, Granddad. Don't mess with me."

"Lightning bugs can't read a calendar, boy... they're shooting their fireworks right now. Look out in the yard!"

I also like to watch the spiders prey on gnats that land on the screens. These black, fluffy jumping spiders have always captured my interest. They appear to skip biting and injecting venom, and instead jump on the gnats and begin to chew. The gnats are probably too little to bite. These little, fuzzy spiders appear to be friendly to me, however the gnats may have a different opinion.

Other spiders construct webs that dangle from the roof's eaves and connect to the porch's posts and screens. With their large, thick abdomen and angular legs, these appear terrifying. They snare in their webs unsuspecting moths and other flying insects that are drawn to the porch light. These spiders seem nasty and evil.

"Granddad, I hate those fat spiders."

"Really? When we mow, I will show you spiders that live in holes in the ground. They are some real monsters!"

"Uh, no thanks."

I once observed one of the fat spiders dangling from a single thread of web, as if it magically hung in mid-air. The spider appeared to be dead; it was motionless and had a contorted body. I assumed it had been sprayed with insect spray and died while attempting to spin its web. When a moth approached the lifeless spider, it jumped and attacked, biting it and rapidly encasing the moth in a straight jacket of web. That spider was faking death, which made me despise it even more. I kill these fat-butted spiders whenever I have the chance.

———

Grandma and Granddad's house has an unusual history. The former owner, a lady, was supposed to be a whiskey bootlegger and all-around scoundrel who lived life on the wild side.

She used to show up at supper time unannounced. She would simply sit in the corner and observe them as they ate. In her mind, the house sale was simply a formality. She was a wary, if not paranoid, lady. They discovered that she had stashed guns, whiskey, and a bunch of cash within the house. My grandparents learned this from the local sheriff, who even revealed the location of certain concealed chambers and false walls where she kept her contraband. She had extensive experience with the law.

"Hey Davy!"

"Yes, Granddad?"

"Do you remember the stories I told you about the bootlegger lady? Well, I want to show you something in my closet. Grab the wood trim on the left side of the door. Pull it hard."

The entire trim popped off in my hand revealing a narrow stack of shelves.

"Whoa!!"

"Davy, I found a Colt .38 revolver in there. I guess the old lady forgot about that secret place."

"This is almost like a haunted house, Granddad! I bet if it could speak, it would have lots of stories to tell. You could make a movie!"

I couldn't get enough of these stories and was always begging Granddad to tell me more. He did not let me down. One of my favorite tales was about their move in day, or should I say weeks. The bootlegger was a hoarder. It took a full two weeks to remove all of her stuff from the residence. The house was filled to the rafters with magazines, brand new clothes, bars of soap that had only been used once, socks and underwear that had only been worn once, and much more. Despite this, the house was immaculately clean. No bugs, bad food, or anything else that might attract rodents. The bootlegger did not help my young grandparents move things out into the backyard, but she kept a strict account of all the items as they passed by.

"Not so fast, young man! Let me see what's in that box you're carrying."

She was on the lookout for something in particular. She didn't seem to find it.

After removing all of the bootlegger's stuff, Grandma and Granddad set about making the house their own. The home has a three-room basement with a workshop. The basement's size made the house appear practically two-storied, three if you considered the attic. The larger basement room contained a full living area as well as beds for guests. The smaller room was turned into a bedroom and a sort of bathroom - I say "sort of" because the bathroom was a closet with a bucket.

It was great fun playing downstairs with cousins away from the adults during the holidays, except when things got out of hand and we started shooting bow and arrows. During our rough play, lampshades and other items were damaged. At other times, we satisfied our curiosity by opening the sleeper sofa, which featured a compartment filled with charcoal sketches of Native American scenery and portraits, a peace pipe, and other intriguing stuff.

I can still hear Grandma say, "Kids, don't get stuck in that sleeper sofa!"

Muffled cries from a cousin as we try to unfold the sofa and get him out...

Somehow she always sensed what we were up to.

There are plenty other things in their home that fascinate me. They do not have central air conditioning, but they do have a swamp cooler and plenty of fans. I enjoy sitting in front of the swamp cooler and letting the cold breeze wash over me. When I'm in the front room, I keep it on high until they tell me to turn it down. It gives a different and more delightful type of cooling than the A/C we had in the city. Granddad always advises me not to stick my fingers in the barrel fan, belt, or wheels.

"Grandson, don't stick your fingers in there," he warns. "They'll get chopped off!"

Because he is missing a portion of his right index finger, I believe he has some experience with finger chopping.

———

I've always liked helping my grandma with the laundry. Her electric clothes ringer fascinates me. It's made up of two hard rubber cylinders that resemble slim rolling pins stacked horizontally on top of each other. When you turn on the machine, the cylinders begin to whirl, grabbing any clothes they can and squeezing all the water out. The clothes are ready to hang on the drying line in the back yard when they come out of the ringer.

To me, the clothes ringer is a mechanical marvel. It beckons me to touch it.

The first time I remember wanting to touch it I was around four years old. I pressed my small fingers against the rotating pins, allowing the slick rubber to spin across my fingertips. However, I got too close to its bite. It pulled my fingers into its crushing jaws, attempting to flatten my bones and squeeze out all of my blood. I couldn't get my hand out of the ringer!

"GRANDMA!!!" I shrieked.

As I screamed in agony, at a blood-curdling pitch, Grandma dashed to flip the reverse switch, and the ringer gradually let go of my fingers. I sobbed on the tile floor.

"I'll never touch the ringer again!"

The fact is, that ringer still tempts me.

When I was little I enjoyed going out back with my grandma and helping her with hanging laundry on a drying line. We had a good time playing hide and seek.

"Peek-a-boo!"

I hid behind and between the sheets, towels, and other clothes drying in the breeze and the sun's warm rays. Everything has an enchantment to it.

———

Now as I look beyond the drying line, I can see what appears to be a grove of trees. They simply call it the orchard. When I move closer the trees, I notice that there is fruit on the branches, which is so heavy that the branches touch the ground. The trees appear to be hunched. Playing in the shade of the trees provides some relief from the Texas heat.

My grandparents occasionally send me to the orchard with a bucket to pick plums, apples, or pears.

"Grandson, wouldn't a pie taste good right now?" adds Granddad. "I'm sure Grandma would bake us a pie if you took that bucket to the orchard and gathered some apples. What do you think?"

"Granddad, that's a no-brainer!" I say.

I'm not particularly good at picking fruit. I always bring back much less than they hope for because I take my time examining the fruit and eating the best pieces. It's fun. And since they are my grandparents, I don't get in too much trouble. And we always manage to have pie!

————

In our new life, Mom is busy taking college classes, working part-time on campus, and commuting back and forth to school, so she doesn't cook much. Grandma spends a lot of time away over this summer visiting relatives and attending family reunions, so the cooking and food preparation fall to my granddad and me. He cooks the meals, while I do the dishes. And let me just say: he's a poor cook. He'd be the first to acknowledge it, I'm sure.

I ask him one time, "Granddad, where did you learn how to cook?"

"When I was young, before I met your Grandma, I worked on a ranch. One of the old hands there taught me how to cook beans 50 ways."

"That explains a lot, Granddad. When is Grandma coming back?"

Grandma can take any assortment of ingredients and turn them into a wonderful homestyle dinner. Her leftovers are simply paint on her palette. She can make an award-winning breakfast out of biscuits and gravy, sausage gravy, homemade jam, pancakes, and omelettes using a variety of ingredients. Her breakfasts are something I miss.

Now, on a regular basis, all we have for breakfast is oatmeal - plain oatmeal. Yuck.

Lentils are a simple meal with a lot of potential, in my opinion. Grandma prepared them with ham and other ingredients, as well as ketchup and rice. Lentils and cornbread make a tasty supper.

But Granddad's lentils are something else entirely. Granddad prepares dinner by boiling them for 20 minutes on the stove with some raw onions.

"Supper is on! Beans #37 tonight!" he would call out.

Let me tell you something: I've always despised onions, ever since someone pranked me with onions in my vanilla ice cream. They are nasty. So when Grandpa serves up lentils with these crunchy, almost raw onions in them, I just can't do it. It is too much.

So I made a daring move one time. I managed to avoid eating the lentils at dinnertime, and then when it was time to do the dishes, I dumped the remaining lentils over the back fence. They could still be there, for all I know. I can't imagine any animal eating that mess.

When Granddad was cooking supper the next day, he said, "Where did those lentils go?"

"I thought we were done with them," I said. "I threw what was left over the fence."

I was aware that I was taking a risk. But I didn't care. Fortunately, he didn't care too much either. Maybe he knew they tasted bad. But we have a constant disagreement over onions. He loves them and believes that I should at the very least appreciate them and be grateful for food.

———

When I was little, my grandparents' property had a hot wire fence out back. It was another source of intrigue for me, primarily because Granddad had repeatedly told me not to touch it. So, what did I want to do? Reach out and touch it. It appeared to be nothing more than a smooth, shiny wire connected to a box in the distance. I was wearing a straw cowboy hat that my Granddad had given me the first time I approached it.

"You should probably wear a straw hat today or you'll get a bad sunburn."

"Okay, Granddad." So I donned my straw hat and went exploring the Ponderosa.

I was roaming around investigating when I came to the back fence. I planned on touching the hot wire fence without actually touching it. So I took off my straw hat and held it out at a safe distance, touching the fence with the brim. I was surprised to feel a strong shock.

"YEEEOOOOWW!"

What I didn't realize was that the straw hat's brim was reinforced with wire to retain its shape. As a result, I was effectively touching the hot wire fence with a wire. I wasn't prepared for it. I thought I'd been transformed into a robot, so I walked back to my grandparents' house in a robotic manner and informed them what had happened to me.

"Grandma, the electric fence shocked and turned me into a robot!"

They laughed and warned me once again.

My curiosity with the hot wire fence was unaffected by this event. I felt like I'd had an adventure. I'd transformed into a robot, and I needed to investigate further. I wasn't dead, and no permanent harm had been done, therefore it was safe to carry out more experiments. I'd heard about boys peeing on hot wire fences, but I wasn't interested. I'm not that daring.

But I did enjoy spending time near it, looking at it, touching it with non-metallic objects, and seeing what happened. And every now and then, when I climbed over or under the fence, I'd get a shock on my back or leg; it was sort of exciting to get shocked by the fence since I knew I wasn't going to die, and even if I did transform into a robot for a little while, it wouldn't last too long.

———

Exploring the land near my grandparents' house was not all fun and games. Summer's heat and humidity were excruciating for an asthmatic child. I love running around the fields behind the home, playing at the pond's edge, picking fruit in the orchard, and doing other things like that, but being around all of that grass always resulted in asthma attacks.

This was a nightmare for me because, when I was little, inhalers had not yet been invented, so whenever I had an asthma attack, I had to take this horrible green medicine. I have no idea what it was called, but it tasted awful and took a long time to work. I've spent countless nights in a rocking chair, battling an asthma attack, holding my head back with my mouth wide open, fighting to breathe, rocking, and waiting for the medicine to kick in. It's pretty scary.

———

Granddad added lawn mowing to my ever-expanding list of tasks. He has one of those self-propelled push mowers, which is cool. But keeping a nice yard so that the neighbors don't make us look bad is a bit of a chore. The neighbor's backyard is a virtual botanic garden. It is green, well-kept, and features a little fish pond with a waterfall. How are we going to compete with that? I'm not sure.

I mow as evenly as I can, but there always seem to be small patches of grass that remain uncut. In his perfectionism, these little strips drive my granddad insane.

He points to the grass strips and exclaims irately, "Do you see this grass? Are you missing something?"

"I'm sorry, Granddad. I'll take care of it."

I believe his annoyance comes primarily from not measuring up to the neighbor's lawn, rather than from my poor mowing.

The fenced-in yard is only about an acre, but by the time I finish mowing it in the sweltering Texas heat, I'm exhausted. I lack stamina. I'll make any excuse to use the restroom or get a cool drink. My grandparents' place has lost some of its charm since I became responsible for taking care of it. I am no longer a beloved guest; I am now a member of the maintenance crew.

The sweltering summer heatwave of 1980 in Texas is difficult to bear in a house without central air conditioning. I can't just spend all of my time in front of the swamp cooler, and fans in other parts of the home provide little relief because they simply circulate the hot, humid air. I routinely report the temperature displayed on the porch thermometer to my mom and grandparents.

"It's 101 in the shade!!!"

I acknowledge that I am a bit self-absorbed, and I am often unaware of what is going on around me. I know I don't really appreciate the fact that my granddad is praying for us. When I'm lying on the couch at 5 a.m. and the rooster starts crowing, he goes outside and prays every day.

His shuffling wakes me frequently, and I watch him go outside. I notice him entering the orchard. I hear murmuring and I know he's talking to God about me and my mom.

———

I really miss Spotty, but he was not the only animal at Granddad and Grandma's house. There are at least 13 barn cats roaming their land. I'm not sure if the cats stay in the barn, but they're around and help the coyotes keep the mouse population in check.

But something changed at one point. Granddad began to notice dead cats and kittens on a regular basis. I won't get into the gory details, but the cats were partially devoured by a predator. Each cat or kitten died in the same way - again, no details.

My granddad begins to see things in the nighttime as our cat population declines. In the evening, it is a custom to take some of the leftovers and throw them over the back fence. My granddad walks out one night to toss out the leftovers for the dogs or anyone else who wants a free dinner when he notices shining eyes in the distance. He suspects that this is not just another dog, cat, or coyote, so he throws out the food and returns to the porch to observe. The beast approaches and consumes everything it desires, primarily the meat. After a few feedings, my granddad notices the type of creature he is dealing with: a bobcat.

Not only does feeding a bobcat in the evenings excite me. It also excites my granddad. In many respects, Granddad is still a child at heart. He starts feeding the bobcat better meals in the evenings, items that should've stayed in the kitchen. We could've used the leftovers for another meal.

"Those pork chops were for lunch tomorrow!!" Grandma catches him a couple of times.

"We could all lose some weight," he replied with a wink.

Grandma was pretty trim, but Granddad not so much...

Granddad is having a good ole time. The bobcat had become comfortable with my granddad by the time we moved in with him and Grandma. Bobby is regularly waiting for the dinner at the fence. Apparently, my granddad's purpose is to domesticate this bobcat. My granddad soon buys a harness and leash for this wild animal. Surprisingly, this bobcat allows my granddad to put the harness and leash on it!

The next thing I know, this cat is in the house with a harness and leash, becoming our house cat - which is incredible in and of itself, considering my grandparents are adamantly opposed to having animals indoors. But this is no ordinary pet.

"Davy, I bet Bobby would like to watch some TV. Do you want to sit with him in my chair and watch a western?"

With Bobby the bobcat splayed out on my lap, I sit in Granddad's rocker-recliner, watching Rawhide on their black-and-white TV. They snap photographs as proof that this marvel truly happened.

To be honest, I'm not sure if Bobby is our pet or if we are his. But it's an incredible relationship that I want to share with others. So, one Saturday, I ask my granddad if I can take Bobby to Sunday school to show the other kids.

"Granddad, can I take Bobby to church today?"

Surprisingly, he says yes without hesitation. Granddad, who has a mischievous streak, would generally leap at the chance to have some fun.

I know other kids have brought things to Sunday School for show and tell, especially if they relate to the topic being taught. I'm not sure what the lesson is next Sunday, but I'm confident we can incorporate a bobcat and make it work. Bobby travels in the back of the station wagon, while the rest of us ride up front.

Bobby is peering out the windows as we drive down the street, taking everything in. He's obviously never been in a car before, so he's a little wired. When he sees other animals like dogs in yards, other cats out and about, and people watering their lawns, he gets fairly frantic and runs around trying to get out. We go straight to the Sunday school room when we arrive at church. We have no idea what is going to happen next.

When the kids walk in, they are both surprised and excited to see a bobcat on a leash.

"Awesome!! Cool!! Is he really yours? How did you do it?!?" The children yell with delight. The energy is palpable.

I feel powerful; I am the man. The teacher begins her class in front of a room full of children and other spectators, but she doesn't get very far.

"Children, isn't it amazing that all of the animals enter the ark so gently with Noah? There are many different creatures, the most of which are probably wild. But God makes them tame, like our guest this morning..."

She speaks too quickly.

Bobby goes berserk.

The Sunday school teacher is wearing a polyester pantsuit rather than a dress. This providentially works for her protection; Bobby goes directly for the teacher and climbs right up that pantsuit, ripping and tearing and going insane.

"AAAAH!!!"

We lunge to pull Bobby off the teacher.

We manage to keep him on the leash, but he runs under tables, between chairs, behind cabinets, and under desks. The children are screaming and laughing, and the teacher is traumatized.

It's fantastic; I've never had so much fun in Sunday School!

Bobby no longer made public appearances. After the church fiasco, he mostly stayed at home. We didn't know that his time was nearing an end. He started going for the neighbors' ducks because he had no cats to eat and was bored with leftovers.

BOOM. We hear a gunshot in the distance.

Bobby the bobcat met his fate at the business end of the neighbor's 12-gauge shotgun. We were saddened by Bobby's death, but we understood.

RIP Bobby.

CHURCH LIFE

M Y GRANDDAD IS A PASTOR, which I was astonished to discover. He is, in fact, the retired pastor of the church
where we worship every Sunday. I've always wondered why
the church members treat him so well. I assumed he was some
type of famous or influential figure, but I had no idea why. He
was a beloved pastor of a Baptist congregation.

My granddad is much more than just an elderly man who
shuffles through the night to use the restroom or cooks unap-
pealing, if not dreadful, meals. In terms of wisdom and direction, I've discovered that my granddad has a lot to teach me.
He is a man who, while small in the sight of the world, is highly
regarded by his fellow believers. He is a man of enormous
spiritual stature who has lived a life of consequence.

Granddad introduced me to rural church life, which is very
different from the large city church I am used to attending.

"Grandson, I'd like to show you around the church and tell
you some stories that you haven't heard before."

Even though the move has been tough, I am willing to go
along with him. I'm looking forward to listening to more of his
stories.

We walked straight up the middle aisle towards the pulpit after entering the church through the front doors. Nothing new here; I walked up the aisle in a similar manner when I professed my faith in Christ years ago. We find ourselves behind the pulpit.

"Look across the pews. Imagine them full of people. How do you feel?" he asked.

"I feel powerful and important!" I said.

"I rarely feel that way when I'm preaching; I feel small, weak, and insecure," he explained. "I am constantly praying and relying on God for the words to say."

That really surprises me, because I have always viewed my granddad as a towering figure even before I knew him to be a pastor. He exudes authority and appears to have all the answers and wisdom anyone could need. I am taken aback when he tells me about his sensation of weakness when preaching and his inadequacy for the job.

"How can such a giant feel so small," I wonder.

He elaborates on what it's like to preach when he looks into people's eyes.

"Sometimes it feels like you are staring down the barrel of a .45," he explains. "Not all the time, but sometimes. You can't keep everyone happy. You have to be both tough and loving at the same time."

He describes it as difficult since he is aware of much of what is going on in the church's life while also being aware of how little is going on in the lives of some church members. It's difficult to preach to people who don't care, because he wants them to care. The issue is caring, and Granddad cares an a lot.

———

First Baptist Church is one of several churches in the small town. There are at least seven churches in town. Everyone in town appears to be affiliated with some, if not all, of the churches. So, if you ask someone what church they belong to or attend, you may receive a lengthy response; there is an ebb and flow between the Methodist Church, the Baptist Church, the Presbyterian Church, the charismatic church, the Pentecostal church, and the other churches that do not fit into any denominational category. People simply move around and switch from church to church; for most people, the church's beliefs are secondary to the friendships, rivalries, conflicts, and scandals.

Granddad describes it this way:

"In the Baptist church, people are born again. If they want more of the Holy Spirit, they go to the charismatic church; if they want to be respected, they go to the Methodist Church."

He never did tell me why people attend the Presbyterian Church; I should ask him.

"In reality, all the churches in town function like one big church, and each church is like a Sunday School class that offers something different with a different teacher in a different style," he continues. "People simply switch Sunday School classes every now and then."

"That, I believe, is how the majority of people feel about the churches."

There is a ministerial alliance in town that meets once a month. They just pray for each other, drink coffee, tell stories, and discuss how to deal with town vagrants and those in need; nothing very spectacular. However, he does mention a Lutheran preacher who smokes like a chimney. That seems hilarious to me. Oh, and the Presbyterian preacher cusses like a sailor.

Granddad probably enjoys telling me stories from his ministerial days because he can't tell them to anyone else. He still lives in the town, and he can't risk word getting out about him discussing confidential matters of the past. Don't get me wrong: he never gives anybody up or tells me anything scandalous. He speaks in generalities, yet with enough detail to keep me entertained. So these stories make up for all of the challenging days spent at his house and sleeping on the sofa. He's still my granddad, and I love him.

———

Folks outside the church who are seeking assistance provide some of the most interesting and safe-to-tell stories. No, I'm not talking about folks who truly need help, but about people who are being shady.

My granddad says that early in his church ministry, he was naive and gullible.

"One time, a couple came to my office seeking assistance," he explains. "Of course, they were asking for money, but I guess they saw someone in me who was eager to give more than money. They were a homeless couple with a puppy. At least, that was their story."

"They needed gas for their vehicle as well as cash. Their story was especially compelling since the man had a hearing impairment that prevented him from working an ordinary job. I offered them monetary assistance from the church budget, and I was ready to send them on their way when they made an unusual request. They asked for help with their laundry."

My granddad replied yes immediately and without hesitation. And, without informing Grandma, he arrived at their home with a large bag of dirty laundry.

"Some needy people came by the church, and I helped them out as much as the budget allowed," he informs Grandma. "But they also asked if I could do their laundry. Would you mind doing it?"

Grandma wasn't thrilled with the prospect.

"I think you can handle it yourself," she said with a sideways glance.

As Granddad loaded the clothes into the machine, he saw odd stuff such as racy underwear and other less-than-conservative attire. He couldn't believe he was actually handling these items.

He laughs and laughs as he tells his story, and I laugh and laugh with him. In retrospect, it's just one of those bizarre tales. It's hilarious, but at the time of the incident, he's just trying to do his job, trying to represent Christ, trying to help others, but naively laying himself out.

Six months later, the same couple returns to town. The man does not have a hearing difficulty this time; instead, he has a speech impediment that makes him difficult to understand. Same dog, same woman, but no laundry.

He tells them he remembers them from months ago.

"I remember you, and your dirty laundry."

"Oh, you must be talking about someone else," they say. "We're visiting for the first time."

They have apparently visited all of the other churches as well. They travel from town to town in that portion of North Texas, preying on good people's gullibility and kindness. People in the church, in their opinion, are suckers to be exploited.

This was one of the many lessons he learned early in his pastorate. People are not always what they appear to be. The "poor" are not necessarily poor. Scammers are plentiful in the world. Granddad came to understand Christ's words, "Be as wise as serpents, but as harmless as doves."

———

Granddad also shares a story about a "healing" that occurred outside the church. One winter morning, he received a call from the nearby café; there was someone in need of help, and they want to send them to the church. This is typical: the Baptist Church is on the front lines. If things don't work out, they go to the Methodist Church. I'm not sure where they go from there.

Anyway, Granddad says, "Sure, send him on."

So here comes this guy on a bicycle, it's freezing outside, and he's only wearing a flimsy jacket. My granddad opens the church door and invites the man into his office.

"Tell me your story, young man," he says.

The man groans and rattles something in his shirt pocket without saying anything.

Granddad thinks to himself, "This is going to be a difficult case."

So, unsure what to do, Granddad hands him a pen and paper, thinking, "Hopefully, this guy can write," and sure enough, he can. He even has excellent penmanship!

On the paper, the man writes, "I need medicine." Then he writes, "I need money for medicine; I am running out."

"What kind of medicine?" Granddad asks again. "Let me look at it."

The man is reluctant to share what he has in his pocket. Again, he is only grunting and writing messages on paper. The man reluctantly lifts his shirt pocket to display the medicine he so badly needs. It's Tylenol.

Granddad realizes he has been conned once more, so he tells the man, "I can give you enough money to get another bottle of Tylenol."

Granddad knows this isn't going to end well, so he walks the man out of his office to the outside of the church and bids him good day. Granddad enters the church, returns to his office, and resumes his studies.

The secretary soon appears at his door, rather concerned. "What is going on?" he inquires. "What's wrong?"

She explains, "You have to come out here; we have a situation. I heard a noise outside and noticed..."

What concerns her is that the man wants to come back in the church, but she is not going to let him; she has locked the door. Granddad looks through the glass door and notices something that would normally take him by surprise. Out on the pavement, the man is speaking fluently; his muteness has vanished. He has been healed! He is no longer in need of that medication.

As Granddad continues to listen and watch, he notices the man taking his bicycle and bashing it against the side of the church. He is not praising God with his words, but rather cursing the church in a very creative way.

Granddad tells me many such stories, about people approaching him after church services and asking for money, about individuals who are really sick and in desperate need of medical attention, or who are at risk of having a heart attack. He frequently sees the same folks the next day in the grocery store, filling up on unhealthy food, sweets, cartons of cigarettes, and other items. It's enough to turn him cynical, yet he manages to avoid it. I'm not sure how.

He receives personal calls from non-church members requesting aid with utility bills, rent, and other necessities.

Ring, ring, ring.

"Hello?"

"Preacher, this is so-and so. I'm in a tough spot. They've cut my power off. Can you help me?"

"Sure, come on by the house and I will help you out."

Some people are smart enough to appeal to Granddad personally, after hours. That way they don't have to be interviewed by the tough little lady at church who manages the benevolence fund. She isn't afraid to ask about those expensive bad habits that people manage to afford, like cigarettes and beer.

That little old lady goes for the jugular every time.

Many times he gives assistance out of his own pocket, since Granddad is a generous person who desires to represent Christ's generosity. He wants to trust everyone, but Grandma has to keep him in check; she is the regulator, the governor, keeping him on track and from going off the rails.

———

Granddad had a tendency to be overly accommodating to others. He related the story of a man who needed counseling, without going into too much detail. The man was standing outside the church with a large pitbull dog. He was clearly distressed and in need of comfort; he needed to speak with someone who would listen to him and console him.

Grandpa was eager to assist.

"Please come inside, young sir. Let's get out of the heat."

The man was about to go inside when Granddad stopped him and said,

"You'll have to leave the dog outside."

Without saying anything, the man gave Granddad a dark stare. It was implied that the man and the dog were inseparable and that if he did not let the dog in, something horrible would happen. It was just a feeling, but Granddad was somewhat familiar with the man's sketchy background.

Granddad hesitantly welcomed the man and his dog into the church and his office. The man was ready to talk, his tongue was loosed, and not everything he said made sense. He related his story, interspersed with weeping. Things became even more interesting when the man asked,

"Can I smoke a cigarette?"

"The cleaning ladies had just cleaned the office," my granddad said after a pause.

The man only responded with a menacing gaze.

Granddad wasn't too terrified of the man, but the big dog was a different story. If the man was not allowed to smoke, several things could have gone wrong: he could have sicced the dog on my granddad, or he could have pulled a knife, or the dog could make a big mess on the carpet.

Finally, the meeting ended. The man felt better and the dog did not make a mess. There were no knife attacks, and the entire counseling session seemed to be a success, except for the smoke that permeated the carpet, couch, and other furniture: the single cigarette that the man had asked to light up turned into nearly two packs in two hours.

Following that, word spread around the church that the preacher smoked. Rumors were difficult to eradicate, especially when the odor of cigarette smoke lingered in the office for months.

———

Granddad says to me as we stand behind the pulpit,

"You know, preaching is, in many ways, the simplest and most enjoyable aspect of being a pastor. Making hospital visits is another simple and rewarding aspect of the job."

Granddad considers hospital visits and funerals to be the most profitable times and occasions. People are at their most vulnerable during these painful times, and Granddad likes to help them. People's hearts are softened, and he can more freely offer the gospel of hope where there is none.

Other aspects of church life are rather inconsequential in the grand scheme of things, but people place a high value on them. The type of carpet used in renovations, the style of singing, the youth ministry and their fun and games, who gets to sing specials in church, how much time is spent on announcements, who controls the kitchen, and even which translation of the Bible is preached from are all examples.

———

Granddad recalls an occasion when he was preaching from the Book of Revelation.

"The gist of that particular sermon was that the times are in God's hands, and people should not be sitting on their hands looking to Heaven for the return of Christ, but rather should be about the business of building the kingdom."

"Everything appears normal as my sermon concludes and the invitation is extended. When Grandma and I get home and sit down for our Sunday lunch, there is a knock at the front door."

"This is unusual," Granddad remarks.

He walks to the door, opens it, and there stands an agitated man - a church member Granddad knows well from previous exchanges. As the member lectures Granddad on the errors of the sermon, the man's smile fades into a grimace and frown.

Granddad apparently has it all wrong, as the man gives him a comprehensive lesson in eschatology. His scowl and frown deepen, and he begins to flush; his lecturing changes into shouting, and his body shakes with rage.

"It would be an understatement to say that this is an unsettling experience for me and your Grandma," Granddad explains.

"I'm a big man, and I'm doing my best to hold it together," Granddad replies, pushing his chest out. "I just want to knock this man out, which I was perfectly capable of doing."

"However, that would clearly exacerbate the situation, so I let this guy say his piece before telling him I am sorry he feels this way. The man seemed to relax a little and wishes us both a good day. He walks out, and I thankfully close the door behind him and return to the Sunday dinner."

The doorbell rings once more.

"I get up hesitantly to open the door and find the same man looking at me again, this time with a big smile," Granddad adds. "What a difference in his demeanor!"

"Oh, I forgot," the cheerful man replies as he extends his hand with an envelope.

"I thank the man and accept the envelope before closing the door. I open it while standing at the door."

"It's a greeting card with the words, *We appreciate you being our pastor. We love and value you.*"

"A crisp, brand-new $100 bill is contained within the card."

"I just earned that hundred-dollar bill!" I tell Grandma.

Granddad goes on, "Let me tell you about some of the people in this church."

We make our way from the front of the church to the back and pause for a bit. He discusses power and responsibility, control and management, and obedience to authority. Then he shows me something extremely amusing.

"What do you see here?" he inquires.

"I don't know," I admit.

He points to the seat cushions in the back pew on the left side of the church, directly against the wall.

"These are old pews that haven't been reupholstered in decades, yet they're still comfortable and in decent condition."

Granddad's pointing makes me chuckle. He asks me what I see and then explains things to me since I don't completely understand.

The cushion of the pew has four smooth indentions side by side.

He says, "These four indentions represent 'butt-print leadership.'"

I can't stop laughing; talking about butts in church is hilarious. This lesson in butt-print leadership will almost certainly never make it into one of his public sermons. This is an impromptu private lesson.

Granddad gestures at the wall near the buttock indentions. Within arm's reach of the pew is the air conditioning thermostat. I'd never noticed it before.

Granddad goes on, "These members are some of the most important, dependable people in the church."

"I'm sure you've heard jokes about the thermostat battle, but these people have complete control. Boyd and Linda are church members who have been attending for nearly 50 years.

Linda has kept the church books for decades, and Boyd has taken care of the property. It's all done on a volunteer basis. And, while many make fun of Boyd and Linda's butt prints, they have served the church with a zeal few can equal."

"Butt-print leadership," Granddad explains, "means being present in your role when you're supposed to be. It involves taking the initiative. It means being visible. It involves maintaining order. It includes keeping everything operating. Boyd and Linda aren't showy, and they're not teachers, but they don't have to be. They are the salt of the earth, and they love to laugh. They are aware of everything that is going on in the church and the community, and they actively lead inside the church by being there at all times. They are dependable and provide stability for this Baptist church."

THE STUDY

BEFORE LIVING WITH MY GRANDDAD and grandma, I always associated life there with the outdoors: the pond, the wildlife, the sunrises and sunsets, the bugs, the spiders, and all of the stories. Except for the swamp cooler, I hadn't given much attention to the life within the house and what it had to offer.

———

Indoor living is a completely other universe in many ways. I discovered Granddad's desk, piled high with books, pieces of paper, pens, pencils, paper clips, and a slew of other office-related trinkets. This is a dream come true for a kid like me.

My mom always informed me that Granddad's study was off-limits. Maybe it's because he spends so much time in there researching and preparing sermons, which I didn't realize at the time. I'm allowed to go in and investigate now since I live there. I suppose it is no longer the sanctum that he knew as a pastor. The books aren't as widely used. Dust accumulates on stacks of paper that haven't been moved in a long time. Granddad still spends time there, though.

I occasionally see him in his study, with the desk lamp turned on, reading his Bible early in the mornings before he goes out to the orchard. Or he's seated in a rocking chair, reading the Bible or another book out loud to himself, with his reading glasses perched on the end of his nose. He is studying and reading more devotionally at this time in his life.

"What are you reading, Granddad?"

"Well, right now I am reading *My Utmost for His Highest* by Oswald Chambers."

"Is it good?"

"It is very good, Grandson."

"I might try it someday."

He desires to be closer to God, which surprises me because I assumed all pastors were already close to God.

One look at him at his desk, the lamps, and the mounds of papers makes me think my granddad is a businessman, even a titan of industry. He *is* a businessman, but it is a different kind of business; his business is heaven. When I stroll through his office, open drawers in his desk, rummage through his documents, and play with his pens, as a 12-year-old I begin to have a more intimate sense of who he is, what he does, and what he has done.

I see names—names of people he is praying for, names of people he has previously prayed for. I see answered prayers, checks by names, and situations that need to be highlighted. What I notice is that my granddad cares about his church. He is dedicated to his work. He is determined to succeed as a pastor, even a retired one. He is serious about being a Godly man. I've got to say that I've never seen anyone like him. In my opinion, he is the source of wisdom. I begin to pay attention to him. I start watching him and observing everything he does. He is completely oblivious of this.

He doesn't know it, but his stumbling through the night past the couch no longer bothers me. His creaky screen door opening at 5 a.m. to go pray in the orchard no longer irritates me.

He winces, "Sorry, Davy. Go back to sleep."

"It's okay, Granddad," I whisper.

————

As much as I enjoy exploring outdoors, I am beginning to explore indoors. I now have access to my granddad's books, even if my books and encyclopedias are still in storage somewhere. And once I start showing interest, he allows me free access to his office and theological library. It doesn't get any better than this for a bookish asthmatic youngster.

I'm not sure if other pastors have libraries, and if so, how big they are and what kinds of literature they have. My granddad, though, must have an unrivaled library, in my opinion. I counted his books once - he has around 2,000. He loved to give me a tour.

"I've collected these books over many years. See that commentary set there? I got that from Grandma's aunt who was a great teacher in her Methodist church."

"And that set there? That is a set of Spurgeon's sermons… the first thing Grandma ever wanted to buy for me. It took a while, but we finally could afford to get it."

"Grab that little ladder if you want to get a closer look."

As I climb the ladder to look at the books, I find unusual volumes; he's got encyclopedias of a different kind, covering archaeology, old languages, metaphors, and commentaries on almost every book in the Bible. Then he has a section of the library dedicated to biography, and another to the writings of other great pastors from the distant past.

"Granddad, have you read all of these books?" I inquire.

"No," he says with a smile, "but I hope to one day."

He definitely has more books than he will ever be able to read, but I can tell that he has read many of them several times. There are books with small tufts of paper sprouting from the top, which serve as bookmarks. It is clear these books are of great interest to him, and I believe they will be to me as well. Some of these books are pretty worn, and some have damaged spines from being opened and set flat on his desk so many times.

Granddad has a habit of writing a date in the front of each book; this date represents the day he finishes the book. The books with blossoming bookmarks have numerous dates scribbled in the front cover - he has read these books many times.

I notice that he has underlined, starred, marked, and commented on the text as I flip through the volumes. This is noteworthy since my mom informs me my granddad is a book purist. He's not one of those preachers who highlights his Bible in rainbow colors and pencils in comments in the margins to the point where the text is virtually illegible. No, his Bibles are normally in good condition, with very minor wear and tear on the outside.

"Granddad, I thought you always said I wasn't supposed to write in books."

He smiled, "Sorry Davy, what I meant was that "you" can't write in my books."

His books all appear to be the same - many of them are very old, but they all look to be in excellent condition, with the exception of the volumes that sprout bookmarks. Granddad is compelled to abandon his purists tendencies by these texts in some way. It's as if he's trying to recall something from the books, commit it to memory, and record it so that it'll be there when his memory fades.

I'm not familiar with the authors of these works; I'm not acquainted with theology, doctrine, or anything else like that. I grew up in churches and am familiar with "Sunday School" answers; I am familiar with the main stories of the Bible. Everyone knows about David and Goliath, and the familiar story of Noah and the flood is etched in my memory, thanks to Vacation Bible School and elderly Sunday School teachers. However, Granddad's library extends beyond the Sunday School curriculum; there is something strange, exotic, and fascinating about his books - many of them have beautiful spines with gold etchings.

The library confirms what I suspect: my granddad is an important person, in possession of advanced and even secret knowledge and wisdom. He is a titan, and I am certain that I am one of the few people who truly understand how special and powerful he is.

———

At my granddad's house, the theological library isn't the only thing that piques my curiosity. I notice that he has an attic as well. A rope hanging from the ceiling in the garage unfolds a ladder when tugged. I spend a considerable amount of time crawling up into the big attic after discovering this. There are boxes everywhere, as well as suitcases, old furniture, lampshades, and so on. I'm not sure how that old furniture got up there; it appears to be too large to pull up the ladder, but it's there. I call this an attic, but it feels more like a room; perhaps there were stairs leading to the attic at one point. It has the feeling of a living room.

I decide to clear some space after repeated trips up to the attic and digging around. A huge, comfortable leather chair is among the many pieces of furniture. It isn't a rocker, which is disappointing, but after dusting it off, it makes an excellent reading chair. There is electricity in the attic, and there are a couple of single bulb lights, so all I need is a reading chair and a light switch to make it my own office.

There is no desk in my office, but there is a coffee table.

"Can I take some of your books that I've been reading up into the attic, Granddad? I want to turn it into my personal reading room!"

The attic provides the privacy I so much desire, as well as a place of retreat.

"You can borrow one or two of my books at a time," Granddad says. "I'm delighted you wish to enter into my literary world. Go for it!"

———

I'll say it again: I hate spiders. And there are spiders in the attic. This is puzzling because I don't notice any flies or other pests up there, but when I start moving the boxes and furniture around, there are spiders. What do they consume? I'm not sure. They look like brown recluse spiders or fiddleback spiders to me. I've seen them before, but not very frequently. I'm aware they're harmful and should be avoided.

They don't reside in holes or webs, but rather in nooks and crannies between sheets of cardboard and in boxes. So I have to be extra cautious when opening boxes and moving stuff around since I don't want to get bitten. When he hears all of that stomping, I'm sure Granddad wonders what's going on. It's spider-killing time in the attic.

I take my time exploring all of the boxes that are up there. What kind of treasure will I come across? There are several suitcases, boxes of old magazines, crates of Christmas ornaments, a fake Christmas tree, some old tools, a box of wooden toys, a cool Lionel train set, a box of old books that don't look like my granddad's, a bag of clothes, a pair of old wingtip shoes, a kerosene lamp, and an old pocket knife.

These are the boxes and items that are visible in the available light. Other things can be seen against the wall beyond the reach of the light bulb, so I'll have to investigate them with a flashlight. So, at this point, I clear the attic floor and position the chair near one of the attic's electric bulbs. I grab a rag and thoroughly dust the coffee table and chair. Then I put the coffee table in front of the chair, and I'm done. This is where I read. This is my workplace. My getaway.

I don't keep anything from my granddad and tell him everything I'm doing. I can see satisfaction on his face because he can sense I'm settling in; it's becoming my home as well as his. Then he does something surprising:

"Come down here, Grandson."

He opens a drawer on his desk and takes a key from it. He leads me to the back of the house to what I mistook for a closet door, and then hands me the key.

"This is your key now. Open the door."

When I do, the door swings open, revealing steep stairs leading to the attic.

"Wow, Granddad. This is fantastic! I thought there must be some steps somewhere! May I have a box of books?"

With a smile, he says yes. I assure him that the bookmarks will not be removed.

The task at hand now is to take inventory of my granddad's library and devise a plan for which books to borrow. I acknowledge my ignorance as I marvel at the new world that is opening up before me.

"Granddad, do you have any recommendations for a 12-year-old boy like myself?"

"You should start with a book by another Baptist preacher named John Bunyan," he suggests. "When he was imprisoned, he penned *The Pilgrim's Progress*. It's an adventure story with loads of action and personalities."

"That sounds good to me!" So I add that book to my list.

"I can recommend some other Bunyan books, as well as *Paradise Lost* by John Milton, *Confessions* by Augustine, and some books by Jonathan Edwards," he continues. "These should keep you busy for quite some time. You will greatly benefit from reading them."

I've never heard of any of these authors, and none of my friends have ever read books like these, but I trust my granddad. He shows me where these books are and assists me in neatly packing them in a box for safe transfer up the stairs into the attic. This is a big leap of faith for my granddad because he is very particular when it comes to his books. The following are the rules:

"No dropping the books, no dog-earing pages, no writing in the books, don't crack the spines, don't open the book more than 90 degrees, don't eat food around the books, don't drink drinks around the books, lay the books flat when done, and return the books to their proper home when you are finished with them."

Granddad is serious about his books!

———

My new reading room is almost finished, but there are still some things in the attic that I haven't explored, particularly the luggage. Three of the suitcases are yellowish-orange in color with leather trim. Except for some odd, leather, multi-colored bowties, the first one I open is almost empty. The second bag contains a panpipe, which is similar to a flute, as well as a fancy harmonica. I'm curious who these belong to and how long they've been in use.

Maybe if I ask Granddad to tell me a story about himself, I'll find out if he's ever been in the circus, or in a quartet, or if he's ever played for money on the streets of any great city - who knows? My imagination is racing with stories and scenarios regarding the history of these musical instruments.

There are also a few old vinyl records by unknown artists. If there's a record player nearby, I'm pretty sure it won't be my type of music - I've never heard of Johnny Horton before, but I'm sure he can't compete with Olivia Newton-John, the Bee Gees, or The Sugarhill Gang. I'm starting to question if these records belong to Granddad and Grandma - they're churchgoers, and this doesn't look like church music to me. Perhaps they were formerly owned by the bootlegger lady. This is something to think about.

I'm also curious about how the heavy furniture got into the attic, and why it doesn't feel like an attic as much as a living space. My thoughts are racing once more. I recall Granddad telling me about the sheriff and how this house has fake walls and hidden rooms.

I find myself nodding, thinking to myself, "Yes, this is cool."

THE YOUTH GROUP

GRANDDAD HASN'T BEEN THE PASTOR of the church for quite a while. The church called a younger pastor after he retired. I never paid attention to the man who followed Granddad because I had never made the connection that he had once been the pastor of the church. But now that I live with Granddad and attend the church on a regular basis, I am more aware of the pastor's Sunday messages, as well as Granddad's responses to him - his private responses, that is.

"Hmm," is his most frequent response to the sermons. Sometimes he says it quietly while the pastor is preaching.

The preacher is humorous and fashionable. He wears bright outfits; I remember one Sunday morning when he preached in a brilliant yellow suit. I don't remember the sermon, but it was probably about keeping a cheerful attitude and turning lemons into lemonade. That's the kind of sermons he preaches: keep everyone smiling, shake every hand, kiss every baby. And he's very good at it.

Everybody loves baby dedications and the new pastor always celebrates newborns as new "members" of the church.

"Hmm."

"Everyone, let's welcome John and Becky's little Ashleigh, the newest member of our church."

During the week, he walks the streets of the little town, chatting with everyone and going by every shop to say hello. Under his direction, the small church is growing in attendance. He is very popular.

I'm not very fond of big church. The worship service that follows Sunday school is commonly call "big church" by the kids. I can't put my finger on it, but in spite of the motivational preaching something is lacking, even for this 12-year-old. My granddad notices it as well, but he prudently keeps much of his criticism to himself.

The youth group, on the other hand, is a different story. When we used to go to church, I noticed that the youth sat in their own area at the front on one side. I had always sat with my parents or grandparents as a visitor up until our move. But now, as a resident and regular attendee of the church, I have the opportunity to join that group and sit with them.

There is a girl named Susan, but everyone calls her Suze. She is the prettiest girl I have ever seen. She has long, curly blonde hair, blue eyes, and a beautiful smile. I always sit one row behind Suze when I'm with the youth group. I can't stop thinking about her. I've never spoken to her, but I know she knows my name because she talked to me once.

She said, "Hi, David."

I read all sorts of meaning into that "Hi."

I imagine myself asking her out for ice cream, playing pinball or miniature golf. I have a huge crush on her. She is a fox. In reality, we only say "Hi" to each other occasionally. She is very popular, and I am not on her radar. But that doesn't discourage me. Oh no.

"Suze will come to her senses and realize that I am the one," I tell myself.

I am confident about that. It is my greatest desire.

When I'm not thinking about Suze, I'm thinking about the youth group's activities. They do a lot of exciting stuff, and their youth minister is so cool. Everyone, young and old, is impressed by his black belt in karate. He performs packed out karate demos in the fellowship hall. He teaches us self-defense and even breaks boards and bricks.

"Hi-YAH!!!"

CRASH, BOOM!!!

"And that's how you fight the devil and purse snatchers."

All in all, the summer of 1980 was fantastic. The church takes us on excursions into the city, to the mall, and to the movies. We even get to see Olivia Newton-John in her new film, *Xanadu.* Church is a blast! The fun never stops.

———

When we moved in with Grandma and Granddad, I had just missed church camp, the great summer event where churches from all over the region congregate for a week of Bible teaching, music, entertainment, Christian comedians, intramural sports, and more. I'm bummed I missed it, but I hope there will be more.

Granddad is aware of my disappointment, but he has some good news for me.

"Grandson, I heard there's going to be another church trip. They're going on a mission trip to South Padre Island this summer."

"Can I go?!? I've never been to an island or seen the ocean!" I eagerly inquire.

"Well, thanks to a generous donor, the cost of the one-week trip has been reduced to $70 per person, which includes breakfast and supper, as well as the accommodations," Granddad brushes his whiskers. "I believe we can swing that!"

"Woo-hoo!! I finally get to go to the ocean!!"

On the day of departure, students crowd around the bus; word of the trip has spread. There are numerous non-church attendees, and we all pile into the bus and take off. It's hot, and there's no air conditioning, but who cares? We'll soon be in the ocean, swimming poolside, eating seafood, and enjoying everything that island life has to offer.

One guy who isn't in the youth group becomes my friend. Ted is his name, and he is pretty smart. He discusses topics that are slightly nerdy and bookish, but interesting in a quirky way. We get along great and decide to hang out during the trip.

We are really excited when we finally arrive to South Padre and our lodging. There are five people per house, winding stairs, beautiful views of the ocean, and white shag carpet—oh, and there is air conditioning!

"Relief!!"

"Crank that thermostat down to 60," Ted yells.

We unload our duffel bags and head to the beach. It isn't entirely what we expected. We must exercise caution since there are thousands upon thousands of blue jellyfish washing up on the beach, and we are warned not to step on them. However, some people are stung. We hurry into the ocean, loving the crashing waves. I wasn't considering that the jellyfish on the beach are in the ocean too!

I envision myself body surfing, whatever that is - I have no idea how to do it, I've only heard about it, but I attempt to perform my own version.

"Hey Ted! Check this out... I'm Dave the Wave!!!

It's a lot of fun; there's a storm out at sea, and some of the waves coming in are rather large. In my attempt to body surf, as I call it, I am hit by a massive wave, which drives me under and rolls me along the bottom, head over heels, till I reach the shallows. It's thrilling, surprising, and a little terrifying, but I want to do it again.

I move out till I am chest deep in the water. I feel something brush up against my leg.

"AAAAHHHHH!!!"

I get scared and swim back to shore. All I can think about is Jaws. I regain my composure and go back out. I'm strolling in waist-deep water when I step into a hole and sink to my shoulders, my feet not hitting the bottom. I panic, my legs are completely cramped, and I can't move.

"HELP ME!!!" I yell to Ted.

Ted simply stands on the beach, laughing.

I'm stuck in a current that's dragging me farther down the beach and out to sea. I'm trying to remain afloat by swimming with my arms. My legs take forever to uncramp, but I manage to escape the tide and swim back to shore. I don't get back in the water for the remainder of the trip; I've had enough, and Ted is not my friend.

———

We are reminded by the leaders that we are supposed to attend evening Bible study. I have no recollection of that ever happening. What I do recall is returning to our hotel and tracking tar from the beach all over the white shag carpet. The youth minister is furious.

"What the heck, guys!?!?" He screams.

"Don't you know you're supposed to take your shoes off at the door? Clean it up right now!"

Ted was first to enter the house. When we saw his black footsteps on the white carpet, we quickly took our shoes off at the tiled entrance. It was too late for Ted, but we all caught the blame.

"Man, Ted! Look at all that mess you tracked in here," I said angrily.

The youth minister makes us scrub the carpet with numerous solutions for several hours in an attempt to remove the tar. I'm very sure the church will forfeit their deposit since we can't get the stains out.

―――――

Our lodgings also have visitors who are not part of our youth group. Suze isn't the only attractive girl; there are older girls sunbathing poolside as well.

"Let's go talk to them," Ted suggests. "I have a plan."

He tells me about his ambitious goals, which I'm sure aren't church-approved. Later, I discover that Ted talks a big game but rarely exhibits his prowess with the ladies.

―――――

There is little to no supervision on this tour, except for the Bible studies at night. The trip's mission activities are elective, putting on concerts at other churches and practicing street evangelism are optional, and most people, including me, opt out. I bring $100 for spending money, which I believe will be sufficient.

The church bus takes us all to a fine restaurant one evening. Before getting off the bus, the youth minister makes an announcement.

"Okay guys and gals, the church will not pay for the meal, so everyone is on their own."

We enter the restaurant an are seated in a large room with elegant table settings.

I don't pay much attention to what other people are ordering, but one item on the menu stands out to me: the seafood platter. I want it all, so that's what I order. It's priced at $17.

I'm a little embarrassed when the dinner arrives, but not too much. The seafood platter exceeded my expectations, with lobster, scallops, shrimp, some kind of fillet, many large hush puppies, clams, oysters, and French fries. It is huge!

"Awesome!" I thought to myself.

Everything is great, except for this annoying girl in the youth group who always behaves like she is in charge, ordering people around and giving unasked for advice. She sits at the next table, her mouth wide open, staring at my seafood platter.

"How? Why? What possessed you to order so much?" she says sarcastically.

I shrug her off.

She ordered a grilled cheese sandwich, while everyone else chose a hamburger or something similar.

I'm the only one who goes all out.

———

The next day or two are busy with optional Bible studies, excursions to different churches, and pranks, some of which should not be mentioned. The typical prank, covering the toilet seat with plastic wrap, is followed by putting Vaseline on a kid's toothbrush.

Not cool.

When that kid got Vaseline in his mouth the next morning, he became furious and got revenge by peeing on the other kid's toothbrush.

Really not cool.

Fortunately, I'm not in the line of fire and am only an innocent bystander.

———

Our youth group mission trip's final day is by far the most thrilling. We all pile onto the bus, which is driven by the youth minister, and cross the border into Mexico. I guess I overlooked the fact that a trip to Mexico was on the itinerary - what a surprise! We cross the border and find ourselves in a huge market, a Mexican bazaar.

"Okay, kids. Listen up! These are the ground rules: You must travel in groups of two or three and return to the bus by 3 p.m. Okay, that's it. Stay safe and have fun! Be back in six hours."

The bus doors swing wide, and kids pour out.

We're in Mexico and we're on our own. So cool!

I'm down to roughly $50. Ted and I are both on top of the world. The vibrant colors, shops, smells, and street vendors are all incredible. Ted and I make our first stop at a knife shop.

"Hold up, let's check out these knives!" Ted says.

The shop owner swiftly seizes our attention to make his pitch. He opens a showcase to display his wares. He takes out a knife, brings it up to our faces, and with a push of a button, a blade pops out. It is a switchblade knife!. I've never seen anything so exciting.

"This is for killing people," the shop owner says with a grin.

I really want the knife, but I can't afford it. He does, however, have gold jewelry. Now we're talking! I'm looking for a necklace. Ted gets one for $20.

The shopkeeper informs us that "these necklaces are pure gold."

They are stunning. I see one I like - a herringbone necklace that is thicker than Ted's.

"Pure gold for 40 bucks!" I exclaim. "They were right - you can get great stuff for cheap in Mexico!!"

Ted and I believe we have struck the deal of the century.

We keep looking around and exploring until we get lost. We find our way back to the bus just as the kids are about to board.

Whew! We all make it out of Mexico alive and well. This is the most exhilarating adventure I've ever taken, and I even make it out with some treasure—a $40 gold necklace.

———

By this point, I'm broke. Breakfast was provided by the church, but lunch on the lengthy journey home was not. I'm starving. When the church bus stops for gas, they let everyone get off to get their own lunch—kids go to Burger King, Mc-Donald's, or whatever else is nearby. Because I don't have any money, I go to the youth minister.

"I'm hungry, but I'm out of money. Can you lend me a few dollars?"

"Here's six dollars," he says with a smile. "Don't worry about it."

"Wow, thank you!" My youth minister is both an expert in karate AND generous! He is so cool.

Ted and I each order a Big Mac and fries to tide us over till we get home.

———

I don't recall much of the trip home, except that it was long and hot. But I don't mind; I've had so much fun. Ted is a nice guy, except that he almost let me drown in the ocean. I'm getting acquainted with some new people and gorgeous girls who aren't from the church. When I say "acquainted," I mean I'm seeing them and learning their names. I'll learn more about them as school begins, because some of them will attend my school.

My new gold necklace occupies most of my thoughts on the way home. I am thrilled. Though I hate the heat, the thought of my cool necklace more than makes up for it. I intend to wear it all the time, including to church.

I notice something about the jewelry a few days after I get home. The area between the links is turning green. In astonishment, I study the necklace. I even take out a magnifying glass to inspect the clasp, which I assumed said 14-karat gold. But it's not 14-karat, it's something else. Even with a magnifying lens, I can't make out the lettering. All I know is that my prized possession is not pure gold.

I'm embarrassed and angry. That shopkeeper lied to me! The $40 "pure gold" necklace was indeed too good to be true. I'm not going to wear that necklace to church or school. And I'm not going to ask about Ted's necklace because I don't want him to ask about mine. It's something I'd like to forget. I should have got the switchblade knife instead.

Yet, overall, I believe this has been a successful trip. It was my first major adventure. I body surfed, almost got swept out to sea, saw beautiful sights, ate the biggest seafood meal of my life, ran wild in a Mexican market, got ripped off by a shopkeeper, saw a switchblade knife for the first time, spent all my money, and made it home on a Big Mac. All in one week!

"Two all-beef patties, special sauce, lettuce, cheese, pickles, onions, on a sesame seed bun."

———

We present a report to the congregation the next Sunday at church. They want to know about our spiritual experiences and growth, as well as how we worship with other churches and offer spiritual encouragement. They want to know about our street outreach, how we were witnesses and represented the church properly, and how the kingdom is progressing. They are interested in hearing about conversions. All of this makes me very nervous.

Fortunately, I am not asked to speak. Those who do share, however, do it eloquently. Other kids may have more spiritual experiences than I do; perhaps they seek it out, whereas I seek out switchblades, gold necklaces, and seafood. Seek and you will find. On this trip, I found what I was seeking for. I doubt the church will ever take youth to South Padre Island again.

The preacher boys in the youth group provide some of the best testimonies about the trip. These guys make me uncomfortable. They appear to be too good to be true. I'm not a bad kid, but I'm also not a "goody two-shoes" either. These preacher boys are so squeaky clean that they are occasionally asked to speak on Sunday evenings. And they are regularly invited to pray.

The pastor likes to ask members of the youth group to lead an offertory prayer or say a benediction. I believe he is attempting to develop leadership qualities among the youth. As the retired pastor's grandson, I somehow fall into the category of "preacher boy" in the pastor's eyes. The pastor unexpectedly calls on me to pray during the service. Panic runs through my body. I instantly go into autopilot mode and repeat a formulaic prayer that is a mash-up of all the prayers I've ever heard before.

When I say "Amen," a kid next to me asks, "Was that a canned prayer or what?"

I look at him and just shrug.

It was totally canned, and I have no idea what I said. Yet, it seems to be satisfactory, because now the pastor frequently asks me to pray.

LAST DAYS OF SUMMER

WITH THE END of summer approaching, all I can think about is having as much fun as possible before the beginning of the school year. I try not to think about starting a new school since it makes me really anxious. I already miss my old school, my friends, the familiar buildings and classrooms, and things I never expected to miss, like irate coaches, cranky custodians, and hard teachers.

The adventure in South Texas and Mexico is difficult to top. However, two avenues of summer fun and satisfaction remain: movies and music. I enjoy watching movies. As far back as I can remember, my parents allowed me go to afternoon matinées by myself. When I was little, I always enjoyed seeing the cartoon shorts before the movies and looked forward to the intermission to refill my Coke and get more popcorn.

The movie theater occasionally shows older films that are sure to draw a crowd. I've seen *The Legend of Boggy Creek* more times than I can remember. I am a huge fan! Bigfoot is so cool! *The Bermuda Triangle* and *The Day of the Dolphin* are some other awesome shows, as well as *Sinbad* and *Jason and the Argonauts*. I've seen so many movies that I've lost count.

Sasquatch, UFOs, and mythological monsters!

In terms of movies, the summer of 1980 is tops! I get to see *Star Wars: The Empire Strikes Back* as well as *Herbie Goes Bananas.* The youth group's last summer outing was to take a busload of kids to the mall and then to see *Xanadu.* To be honest, I can't think of a finer church outing than seeing an Olivia Newton-John movie!

The rest of the summer is riding around bicycles with my new friends. Ted, who does not attend my church, becomes a constant companion for the remainder of the summer. The nearest movie theater is around five miles from where we live. A tractor supply store with a pop machine is about halfway between home and the theater.

So, on hot summer days, Ted and I ride to the tractor supply store for a pop, then to the movie theater for a matinée. We head home after the movie, and if we have any money left over, we stop by the tractor supply store again and buy another pop.

"Hey Ted, who would win in a fight, Bigfoot or that cave monster on Hoth?"

"That's kind of like a grizzly bear fighting a polar bear! My money is on the Hoth monster!"

Ted's a smart guy.

———

This summer, I'm getting more interested in music. The kids at church listen to Christian music, and I hear them talk about Keith Green, Amy Grant, BJ Thomas, and The Imperials. I have an 8-track stereo and listen to edgy music, like the Beach Boys.

My mom observes all of this and does something really cool: she buys me a Sony Walkman. She also buys a bunch of Christian music cassettes for me so that I can keep up with the other kids in the youth group. I feel on top of the world as I ride my banana seat bike around the little town while listening to my Walkman.

I'm so happy.

THE NEW SCHOOL

SUMMER'S HAPPINESS AND CAREFREE pace are fading; in a few days, I will start a new school. As I approach seventh grade, I am more aware of not only music but also of my own and other people's changing bodies. Suze is on my mind. My interest in girls is growing.

The bus arrives at my grandparents' house on the first day of school. I don't think a bus has ever pulled up to this house before, at least not in decades; they might have had to create a new bus route just to come pick me up. I'm apparently one of the first on the route, so when I get on the bus, there are only a few of kids there. I sit near the front of the bus since I've heard horrible things happen at the back. In reality, I'm not sure. I've just seen stuff on TV and in movies. I enjoy sitting in the front, just behind the driver. If I lean down, I can see what the driver sees and check out all of the passengers in the mirror.

Several kids board the bus at each stop. They clearly have ridden this bus many times before, and they all have their preferred seats. I'm wondering if I'm sitting in someone's seat as I watch these strange faces board the bus.

I hold my breath. But as the seats fill up, my mind relaxes a little; I guess no one wants to sit directly behind the driver, which is fine with me.

I don't know where to go when the bus arrives at the school, so I just follow the crowd. They take me to the gym, where I see a large number of students seated on the bleachers. I hear kids calling out my name as I walk into the gym. I discover that everyone is aware that the old preacher's grandson will be a new student this year.

I've never lived in a small town before, so I'm not used to everyone knowing everything about me; there is no anonymity in this town or at school. I recognize several faces from the church youth group, but Suze's face makes me the happiest. As I walk inside the gym, she notices me and waves.

"Hi, David!"

My heart begins to rush; Suze is older than me, so she will be in a different grade, but her presence at school thrills me.

I'm invited to sit with a bunch of kids I know from church.

"Hey, look over here! Come sit with us."

As I walk over, I notice that they are laughing and talking energetically about something. They introduce me to Jerry and Kent who appear to be friendly. I'd seen Kent at church before, but Jerry was new to me. Jerry appears to be popular and the center of attention.

"Check this out!" Jerry exclaims.

He opens his mouth to show me where he had a tooth pulled.

When I look closely, I notice a hole in his lower jaw where a tooth used to be. He breathes hard on me just as I'm looking in his mouth. His breath stinks and the kids laugh as I gag. I'm at a loss for words. Their conversation shifts to other topics, such as basketball.

We stay in the gym until the bell rings for school to begin. We're supposed to stay on the bleachers until the bell, but once the monitor steps out someone snatches one of the basketballs and starts shooting baskets.

"I bet you can't make a half court shot!"

"Just watch me!!"

He shoots. Nothing but net! Kids go crazy.

They don't seem to get in too much trouble, and don't seem to mind getting caught. They love seeing the monitor get frustrated and angry.

———

Sports are very important at school. I know I'll never be a football player, I have looked in the mirror, but basketball is a possibility. As I eventually discover, there are basically three groups of people at the school: jocks, stoners, and cowboys. Of course, it isn't that simple, but these are the major groupings of people who comprise the student body. I'm not a stoner or a cowboy, so could I be a jock? I'm not certain. Cowboys can be jocks, and jocks can be cowboys, but I don't know any stoners that are either.

There are other smaller groups of kids, such as the nerds. It doesn't matter if I consider myself a jock; what counts is how others see me. So I've realized that being a bench-warming athlete who never gets to play in a basketball game is better than being labeled a nerd.

"Want to play chess with us? We have a tournament going on."

"Uh, no thanks." I smile politely.

I choose sports since athletics are the primary focus at school, with academics coming in a distant second. I enjoy basketball and fantasize about dunking the ball. I enjoy watching Dr. J and the Philadelphia 76ers, so joining the basketball team seemed to be the way to go for me. Everyone tries out for the squad, and if there are enough jerseys, you will make the team.

It was a real plus if your jersey fit right.

"Hey Randy, your top is kind of tight! Ha ha ha!!" they laughed at the overweight boy.

"Good thing I'm skinny!" I said to myself.

People who get actual playtime, in my view, are outstanding. Bryan, a star player, outperforms everyone in terms of ability and effort. He practices in the gym before and after school, as well as on Saturdays. His natural skills are impressive; as an eighth grader, he can practically dunk the basketball. He is graceful and swift, and he can think on his feet while playing.

"Nobody can beat us this year," coach says, "cause we've got Bryan."

"State, here we come!"

Others compensate for a lack of natural talent with grit, persistence, and even meanness. James is the team's other outstanding player. He is feared because he fouls aggressively and isn't scared to get kicked out of a game.

He also enjoys fighting after school. Many kids see the after-school slugfests as just another sport, even though they are not sanctioned by the school. These fights take place after school on an empty lot several blocks away.

We have basketball practice every day and it consists of running laps around the gym, wind sprints, and ball-handling drills. My asthma frequently interferes with my running, and I even passed out once. I'm the skinny kid with the puffer. The ball-handling drills aren't going so well because I'm not very coordinated. And my bench-warming status is confirmed when it comes to analyzing the plays and running them on the court.

"I thought you were a straight A student! What's wrong with you? What do you not understand? Get your head in the game!!!"

I hate it when the coach yells at me in front of everyone; as a basketball player, I'm a bit of a slow learner.

But I've discovered that you can be a valuable member of the squad even if you don't play. You can be cool in the locker room if you wear the right shoes and use the right deodorant. I know kids who wear the shoes and use underarm deodorant and are content to sit on the bench. These are the tools of a great athlete.

Right Guard to the rescue! The least expensive and most effective path to coolness. The locker room was fogged every day after practice with aerosol spray deodorant.

There are other kids that join the squad but never play, never wear cool shoes, and, based on their odor, never wear deodorant. I'm thinking of one particular person, whose name is Doug. I'm afraid of him. He takes meanness to a new level; he is a terror. One time I saw him with a rope around his neck, tied to a railing in front of the bleachers.

"Hey!" exclaimed Doug. "Look at this!!"

He leaps from the bleachers over the railing, as if attempting to hang himself. There is about a foot or less of slack rope when he hits the floor; if it was any shorter, he would break his neck. The seventh graders are terrified by his pranks.

For seventh graders, the locker room is a source of great anxiety, primarily because we know that the initiation is near.

We've heard a lot of stories, and we're scared. Most of the stories, I feel, are made up; they never happened. Nonetheless, I see one initiation rite that leaves us scarred for a long time. I won't get into specifics, except to mention that it involves the older boys and Doug humiliating a seventh grader.

"Ohhh, eeww," the onlookers winced and groaned as they witnessed the initiation.

I got out of there as quickly as I could.

All of the wild stories about initiation rites, Doug's terrors, and the overall intimidation that some of us feel in the locker room are pretty normal. No real harm is intended. The upper-classmen just want to have some fun. The older boys, for the most part, are friendly. They are trustworthy, and they usually come from good homes. Otherwise, they would be barred from joining the squad. Still, I'm surrounded by guys with facial hair, muscular arms, and strong legs. I just hope no one forces us to take group showers.

Ted and I see *My Bodyguard* at a Saturday matinée soon after the fall semester begins. It would be cool if I had my own bodyguard; a friend large and strong who could kick butt. It's far-fetched, but it's fun to dream about. The fear and intimidation in the locker room diminish as the season progresses, and the older players begin to focus on the game and running plays, as they all want to make it to the state tournament.

———

Hard rock music was another thing I discovered at school. I don't think I ever heard it at church. I'll be the first to admit that I prefer rock music over the Christian music kids listen to at church. In the gym one of the players turns on his boombox during practice, which I think is okay with the coach.

I remember this kid vividly because he shoots and makes 100 free throws in a row - it's incredible!

With each swish of the net the team chants, "97, 98, 99...!!"

The entire time he is shooting the boombox is blasting a band that I have never heard before. They speak to me; they are visceral and even inspirational. AC/DC's *Back in Black* is the song.

That song makes me feel like I can do anything. As a spindly kid who feels completely weak and intimidated in the locker room but loves the sport, if I listen to the music enough, I'll be able to stand up, become a top player, and dunk on James, Doug, or anyone else.

At the same time, I'm aware that this song contains something forbidden. I know it's wrong, but it feels so right. I'm sure my mom and grandparents would not approve, yet this music speaks to me. It gives me the confidence to push back and overcome because it makes me feel powerful and strong. It's so daring and rebellious. I think it's brilliant.

I soon learn about the Fellowship of Christian Athletes (FCA). We meet after school and are sponsored by a teacher. All of the good kids go. I recall at least one meeting, if not more, dedicated to the evils of rock 'n' roll, particularly what they call "backward masking." The aim is to play a record backwards and listen for the devil's secret messages. These vinyl records contain a demonic message, so when you listen to them forwards, the songs sound normal, but your brain will also comprehend the subliminal reverse message. We get a lot of lessons and demonstrations about the devil and rock 'n' roll.

The worst offender, as far as I recall, is Led Zeppelin. The meetings conclude with everyone going to an off-campus location to burn their records, tapes, and cassettes. I never take part in these burnings because I'm pretty sure the Beach Boys don't perform backward masking, and I'm not sure about Led Zeppelin either. I don't go to FCA meetings very often because they are after school and I typically have to find a ride.

———

The school library is another great thing I discovered. I am a huge fan of libraries! When I was in third grade, the bookmobile would come by, and it was so much fun to get on the bus and check out books. I recall it vividly - a mobile library, how fantastic! I am at home in the library. My buddies - books - supply what's lacking for me in the classroom, locker room, and on the court.

The school library is where I come across *The Lord of the Rings*. Tolkien is more satisfying to me than AC/DC. After discovering these books, I devoured *The Hobbit, The Fellowship of the Ring, The Two Towers*, and *The Return of the King*. I even tried to read *The Silmarillion*. I ended up reading *The Lord of the Rings* seven times. As I don't totally fit in with the jocks, I'm beginning to recognize myself as "bookish." Off the court and outside the classroom, my voyage of self-discovery, the finding of my bookish-self, continues.

My new school has an open campus during lunch, which means I don't have to eat in the cafeteria; instead, I can stroll down to the convenience store and get something to eat.

Ted, "What are you buying for lunch today?"

"Mustard sardines and a cream cheese danish!"

I make sure that the allowance that my granddad gives me is well spent.

For those that live nearby, they can just go home and eat. Lunch lasts about 30 minutes, and many students use the open campus lunch period to socialize rather than eat. Jon invites me to his place with some other boys, and he does it with a smirk.

"Come along with us if you want to have some cool fun."

They ask me to join them in smoking some marijuana, but I politely decline. I'm not going to be their entertainment, and I'm not going to get in trouble. The stoners, as friendly as they appear to be, are not my type.

———

Aside from sports, there are other new aspects of seventh grade. I no longer have a homeroom teacher, and each class is in a different room. Miss Smithfield teaches English, Mrs. Rose teaches Geometry, Mr. Carland teaches Art, and so forth.

Each student has their own locker and must provide their own lock. It's important to have the right type of lock. Combination locks are way more cool than key locks. I'm making a mental list of the stuff I'll need to be cool: Aerosol deodorant, yes. Cool tennis shoes, yes. Combination lock, yes. How much more do I need? I have to remain on top of this. Things are getting stressful. My anxiety is rising.

For a variety of reasons, English is my favorite class. First and foremost, it's pretty easy. I am good at grammar and don't need to study very hard, if at all. Furthermore, English is combined with literature, so we get to read stories and take quizzes on them. Miss Smithfield, our English teacher, is the second reason I love English. She reads to us; sometimes selections from Charles Dickens, other times entire novels. She is currently reading *A Wrinkle in Time*, which I love. Miss Smithfield is about 21 years old and just out of college. All the boys love her. She seems to have stepped straight off the set of Charlie's Angels, with her blonde, feathered hair - all the guys obsess over her. I'm sure she's aware of the fact that almost every boy in school has a crush on her. She is popular and so nice.

She occasionally assigns writing projects. It is customary for her to pick up the papers and read selected essays. In her class, my thoughts alternate between Suze and Miss Smithfield. Typically, the teacher provides essay prompts. But one day, she told us we can write a short on any subject.

"Students, take out a sheet of paper and write your name on it. Your assignment today is to write a 500 word essay on any topic of your choice. Be creative. Just keep it appropriate. You have 30 minutes."

I immediately started writing an essay about the characteristics of my dream girlfriend. Without thinking, I simply picked the low-hanging fruit that was on my mind at the time. I take my time writing the title, introduction, body, and conclusion.

As is frequently the case, I submit my essay before everyone else. But I shouldn't have done that. Miss Smithfield sits there silently reading my essay as I finish it ahead of everyone else. As the other kids turn in their essays, she carefully stacks them on her desk, but she keeps mine separate.

I don't think much about it; in fact, the entire incident demonstrates that I don't think much at all. She walks over to her stool, where she typically reads to us, once the final person has turned in their completed essay. She only has one essay in her hands, and it is the first one she has received - mine. Oh no!

I bury my head in my hands, groan audibly, and give Miss Smithfield a pleading look.

The worst-case scenario occurs. In front of the entire class, she reads my essay. Everyone knows what my dream girlfriend looks like; they are aware of her mental attributes, physical appearance, interests, athleticism, and other characteristics.

Essentially, what they hear is a mash-up of Miss Smithfield and Suze. I'm horrified; I believe Miss Smithfield intends to humiliate me, and she succeeds. It's not that I'm thinking any differently from the other guys; it's just that I wrote my thoughts down. I feel betrayed by the teacher. But I should've known better; she's young, and I'm sure she's just wanted to have some fun.

———

Mrs. Rose is a geometry teacher who is elderly, sarcastic, and not particularly nice or popular. Because geometry follows English, we have to transition from the beauty to the beast. I'm on the second row, in front of a guy named Steve.

Steve is a bit of a mystery; he doesn't say much and is easily angered. We share the fact that both of our parents are divorced. Steve is a big, strong guy, and I hate guarding him on the basketball court because, like James, he loves to foul.

I don't know how to say no when Steve asks me to lean over to the side when we are taking a test.

Mrs. Rose distributes the geometry test row by row before instructing us to begin. I lean to one side as I take the test so that Steve can see what I'm writing. Mrs. Rose summons us up to the front of the class after we turn in our tests.

"Boys, I noticed something odd about your papers. Your answers are identical."

"Someone has been cheating."

I just look at her blankly and act as if I don't understand what she's saying, not even glancing at Steve. Of course, Steve is seated behind me, and the cheating can only occur if he looks at my test. Fortunately, we only get a warning. Steve never asks me to lean over again, and even if he did, I have no intention of doing so. I don't want to make the same mistake twice.

———

I had always been a teacher's pet at my previous school. Mrs. Burns would bring me up to the front of the class every day and give me a big hug; third grade was particularly wonderful. She would summon me to the front when it was time to line up for lunch or recess.

"David, please come up to the front of the line."

Big squeeze from the teacher.

Normally I would think it was weird to be hugged that way every day, but somehow with Mrs. Burns it was alright.

I had no idea what the other kids were thinking, but I loved Mrs. Burns, who appeared to adore me. She lived down the street and rode her bike to school every day.

Sixth grade was also memorable due to the fact that I rarely completed my coursework and never turned in an assignment. There was an awards ceremony at the end of the year, and I received the Best Citizenship Award - go figure!

So that's what I was used to: teachers who adored me and treated me as if I were their favorite. But there was none of that at this new school. Seventh grade is not off to a good start. Cheating, humiliation, coaches yelling at me, drug invitations, and more; the pressures are mounting, and I am becoming increasingly insecure and lonely.

I haven't formed any deep friendships at church, and Ted is all I have at school - and I'm not too sure about Ted. Ted appears to be what my granddad refers to as a "fair-weather" friend, meaning that if the church is doing anything interesting, going somewhere fun, or whatever, Ted is there.

Ted is my "good times buddy," but he's also the person who pulled my gym shorts down to my knees in front of all the girls during basketball practice - it was all a huge joke to him. What evens things out between me and Ted is that I know he likes Barry Manilow; with that information, I can take him down. It would be worse than having his gym shorts yanked down in front of the girls if everyone knew he loved Manilow.

––––––

I also have Reading class. This course is intended to improve reading speed and comprehension. Every single day is a race. We have these small projectors that we load with film strips; each frame contains one, two, or three words. We turn on the projector and the words flash quickly on a small screen in our cubicle. The projector features a dial that controls how quickly the words appear on the screen. The goal is to read as quickly as possible while maintaining 100% comprehension. I can read 2000 words per minute on easier material, but my speed drops to 750 words per minute on more challenging material. I am pretty happy with myself, especially when they inform me that I am reading at the 11th or 12th grade level. Of course, this means nothing to the jocks, cowboys, or stoners. They don't care; this is a bookish thing that gives me pride, comfort, and affirmation.

I'm called out into the hall one day and informed that the administration wants to give me a test.

"David, we have been monitoring your performance in this class, as well as your others. Would you like to take a test for a special program we are launching here at school?"

"Sure," I replied tentatively.

The test entails listening to long sequences of numbers and then repeating them backwards, as well as solving puzzles with geometric forms and other activities. Later, I learn that I will be enrolled in a gifted and talented program and will attend special classes.

One of the classes is advanced math, which I despise. There is only one other student in this class, and he excels in math and enjoys it. The teacher gives me an exam, which I fail. She is stunned.

"David, I am surprised that you failed this test! Are you not feeling well? Let's review the test, then you can take it again."

So she gives me the same test again so I can correct the problems I missed.

Another special class is a higher level physics course, which I believe is comparable to math. I'm not sure how I'll do in that class, but I like the teacher because he's one of the school's coaches, as well as my Sunday school teacher at church. He tells many stories of his youth. He had a rough upbringing, frequently fighting with his siblings, and was once stabbed in the back of the hand with a fork by a younger brother.

"Keep your hands off my bacon!"

———

Pranks and stunts are not limited to the gym or the locker room; they also occur in the classroom. I've heard of several pranks from the past, such as putting a cow on top of the school building. I'm not sure how that is possible. I have, however, witnessed a couple pranks. Someone once unscrewed the chalkboard and left it dangling from the wall, and when the teacher began writing on it, the entire board crashed on her.

Fortunately, she was not injured, but she was fuming with anger.

"WHO DID THIS?! WHO DID THIS?!?"

The students burst out laughing.

Another frequent prank is filling out a large number of trial magazine subscription cards for a targeted teacher or coach. Unsolicited magazines begin to pile up in their mailbox, and bills soon follow. I experienced this firsthand when someone subscribed my granddad to some dirty magazines. Having those magazines arrive in the mailbox was extremely awkward. Of course, he got rid of them quickly, but you know how people in small towns talk.

———

The biggest prank of all time remains the most daring and revolting. Someone is writing graffiti in the boys restroom - using poop. The perpetrator is unknown; it's a mystery how he does what he does, especially considering the breaks between classes are only around five minutes long. During that five minutes, though, some junior high or high school boy (we're not sure) goes to the restroom and makes works of art within the stalls.

I was perplexed the first time I saw something like this; there was a neat square of poop stuck to the stall's inside wall. I wasn't sure what to think; what would drive someone to do something like this? Nobody knows. However, the villain grows bolder as his abstract shapes transform into genuine graffiti. I'm sure the offender is known to some of the other boys, because they must keep watch while the perpetrator crafts his masterpieces.

I asked Ted, "Do you know who this is?"

I thought Ted, who was pretty clever and seemed to always have the inside scoop, would know.

"They call him The Poop Artist. That's all I know," he said in a low voice.

The teachers and administration are baffled as to the identity of the person vandalizing the facilities in such a disgusting manner. What about the custodians? They're completely out of their minds; it's one thing to fix a clogged toilet, but it's quite another to clean a mess off the walls of a bathroom stall.

Using the process of elimination, teachers and administration try to figure out who is in the bathroom around the time the discoveries are made, which classes are on break, and which students have a reputation or temperament that might lead to such behavior.

The Poop Artist's celebrity grows over time. Is he a hero or a villain? Will he ever be found? What will happen if he is discovered? Will he be praised or condemned? The fall semester at our school has already become legendary.

Someone is even selling t-shirts that say, "Poop Artist for President."

One afternoon, several guys went to the bathroom at the same time between classes. It was nothing out of the ordinary; I'm there too. People are harassing those in the stalls, pounding on the doors, some are having water fights, while others are just hanging out, treating it like an office and having important conversations.

The custodians always arrive at some time later in the day to clean up whatever mess was made. This time, the custodian arrives immediately after the bell rings. So as the boys file out of the bathroom, the custodian is ready to enter with a mop bucket and other cleaning supplies. The boys are surprised, but they continue on their way back to class.

As the custodian enters the restroom, he hears someone in one of the stalls.

"It's time to get to class," the custodian warns. "I need to clean up in here."

He notices that one of the stall doors is closed, which is where the noise is coming from. He dashes over and peers through the crack. What does he notice? He notices Doug, who is caught in the act. Doug is the kid who ties a rope around his neck and leaps from the bleachers. Doug, the kid who takes part in the locker room initiation rites. Doug is at work as The Poop Artist. Doug is caught red-handed. But his hands aren't red.

The custodian begins to yell at Doug, "GET OUT!!"

Doug dashes to class as the stall door flies open.

This is brought to the attention of the principal, who locates Doug and orders him to clean up the entire mess.

The mystery of The Poop Artist has been solved.

———

During the first few weeks of school, my anxiety skyrockets. I'm not being treated the way I'm used to, and I'm in some kind of gifted program. This is fine, but it separates me from the other kids. I'm not very good at basketball, I don't have the most fashionable shoes, and I can't ask my mom for extra aerosol deodorant because it's not in our budget.

I'm the new kid, and I'm pegged as a preacher's kid. That alone puts me in a different category; I'm not supposed to curse, smoke weed, or listen to rock music. I'm referred to as the goody-two-shoes church kid. I don't want to be bad, but I do want to be accepted. I have no idea how to navigate this new environment. The youth group at church appears to be more welcoming, but I'm not really sure.

To make matters worse, my crush on Suze is growing stronger. We rarely talk, but I quickly discover that she lives just one bus stop away. She doesn't take the bus every day because her older brother occasionally drives her to school. But she will, from time to time, board the bus and she sits next me occasionally. She is two years older than me. My face has been breaking out with pimples since the summer. Acne, yet another source of anxiety, is rearing its ugly head.

School isn't hard, especially if I remember to keep my thoughts to myself when writing essays. I rarely have home-work. I usually go home and pick up a book to read after surviving a day of basketball practice, the locker room, the bathroom chaos, and the school cafeteria food.

The books I read are sometimes from my granddad's library and sometimes from the school library. I start to take Grand-dad's reading recommendations seriously. My safe haven, my refuge is up in the attic, in that nice old leather chair. I'm free to be myself there. The only navigation I have to worry about is flipping through the pages of a thick book.

As unpleasant as it is to live in someone else's home, and knowing that my mom has her own world of stress, I still feel safest at Grandma and Granddad's place.

THE BOOKS

I'M NOT SURE HOW LONG it will be before I feel like I belong at school. Thankfully, I've discovered that Granddad's library is my place of peace. He told me that it is also his haven. I think it's wonderful that we share the same retreat. Granddad is becoming a mentor and even a friend. I can chat with him and he listens to me as if I'm the only one on the planet. That, I suppose, is what makes him a good pastor. He is a great listener.

I began telling him about what was going on at school, as well as some of my concerns and anxieties, such as not fitting in with the other kids.

"Follow God and seek the kingdom first," he advises. "If you do that, everything else will fall into place at the appropriate time."

Granddad is wise. I'm sure he's not perfect, but in comparison to some of the wild stuff I've witnessed at school, he's an angel.

"Go back to the books," he instructed.

So I go upstairs, open the carefully packed box, sit in the big chair, and begin flipping through some of the volumes. I'm a reader, but these books are on a whole new level, and I'm not sure I'm up to the challenge. He told me, perhaps to console or reassure me, that I could build stamina as he did when he first met Jonathan Edwards.

He described picking up Edwards' book *Freedom of the Will* and reading it from front to back.

"Davy boy," he said, "I felt like I was drowning when I first started reading Jonathan Edwards. It was a completely overwhelming experience."

I crack open Edwards to see what all the fuss is about. I count the words in one of his sentences and discover that it contains 200. Yikes!

So I put Edwards down and pick up Milton. I'm not a big fan of poetry, so when I start reading *Paradise Lost,* the longest poem I've ever seen... No, thank you. Then I pick up John Bunyan's *The Pilgrim's Progress.* This appears more readable. There's a lot of dialog and, as Granddad stated, it appears to have some action. But, with so many 'thees' and 'thous,' the book could be a challenge as well.

There are some other books in the box that Granddad had selected, and I go through them as well, but nothing really grabs my attention or strikes the right chord for me. But then I come upon a book that appears to be interesting: *Jonathan Edwards' Images of Divine Things,* edited by Perry Miller. On page 34, Granddad had highlighted a passage.

> The world of these things, sun, moon, stars, and singing birds, is still for Edwards, as it was for Augustine and Calvin, mutable and corruptible. Yet their real being is not in mutability or corruption; it is in the metaphysical realities of which they are the shadows. Edwards' contention is that the metaphys-

ical realities, though capable of abstract statement, exist only in the infinite shadows of the physical world, where intelligence, if it is pure, may read them as naked ideas. Nature thus interpreted becomes a principle of activity; the perceiving mind, taken in a completely empirical sense as wholly "passive," participates in matter as a voluntary intention. *Human intelligence, the image of the intelligence that informs nature, finds in mutability not a mass of confused appearances but analogical traces of the deep realities, the intentions of God. Human perception of these analogies is the human response to divine conversation.* A man who sets himself to reason without divine light is like a man who, going into a garden at night, compares things together by feeling his way from plant to plant and measuring the distances: "But he who sees by divine light is like a man that views the garden when the sun shines upon it. There is, as it were, a light cast upon the ideas of spiritual things in the mind of the believer which makes them appear clear and real which before were but faint obscure representations."

Granddad talks about divine light and nature; he is a deeply spiritual man. I'm not sure if all preachers are like this, but he talks with God. He spends a lot of time outside first thing in the morning, especially when he goes into the orchard. So when I read these highlighted phrases in this book about a human response to a heavenly discussion, along with deep realities in nature and shadows in the physical world, it reminds me of *The Lord of the Rings* or something along those lines.

I keep flipping through the book and discover that it is a notebook, diary, or journal. Edwards writes about fish, stars, caverns, clothing, grasshoppers, gravity, fire, corn, blossoms, trees, tall structures, Judgment Day, owls, venomous creatures, machinery, and many other topics.

The book is rather easy to read and certainly engaging, so I decide that this is where I should begin. I go up to the attic after school most days, climb into the chair, get as comfortable as I can, and crack open this book. The attic is hot, no matter how nice the chair is. Granddad has a box fan and an extension cord that he lets me borrow. Things become somewhat more pleasant after I have some air circulating in the attic, and I can concentrate more on reading.

I do more than just read in the attic; there are still things to discover. I can see outlines of boxes against the wall just beyond the light emitted by the bulb. I need to go through these boxes; who knows, maybe I'll find a treasure or something significant. I decide to drag one of the boxes into the light, dreaming about the possibilities within each one. I glimpse the glitter of something within when I begin to open a box. As I open it all the way, spiders begin to crawl out. I completely freak out; Grandma, Granddad and Mom are surely thinking the roof is collapsing!

"What is going on up there?!?!?" they yell.

"SPIDERS!!!"

I return the box, praying there aren't any other filthy spiders in there. When I'm convinced I've killed all the spiders, I give a double stomp to any who are still writhing. More books are discovered in the box, but they are not from Granddad's library and do not appear to be particularly fascinating.

The thing that I noticed glimmer or glint in the light is on top of the books. It's a set of vintage spectacles or reading glasses. This is exactly the kind of treasure I was hoping to discover! I place them on the coffee table, move the box out of the way, and kick all the dead spiders out of my sight with my foot. I'll have to ask Granddad for some insect spray or something to kill the spiders...creepy.

I am aware that I am different. At least, I believe I am. I don't know anyone at school or church that share my interests. It appears that imagination plays a larger role in my life than in the lives of other kids, or that they must imagine different things. But I can't be alone, because many people enjoy *Star Wars*. People I know enjoy *The Lord of the Rings, The Hobbit,* and Tolkien. I can't be the only one who is worried or insecure. I know that school, sports, girls, teachers, and bullies must cause anxiety in other people. But I do feel isolated.

I'm disturbed by vague concerns that I can't put my finger on. Recently I was lying in bed at night, staring up at the ceiling, and I felt like something was in the room with me. I felt frozen and as though something was laughing at me. The room was completely dark. It was a horrible experience. I just kept praying till the terror passed and I could finally sleep. These things never happened at my previous school.

However, a lot has changed. Mom is still very worried. I know she is concerned about the uncertainty of life and hopes for everything to go well. All I want to do at the age of 12 is to get away. I'm already sick of life. I want to travel to Middle-earth or another magical land. Stress is taking hold on me. I'm too young to grow up. I yearn for a carefree existence that seems far out of my reach.

I can recall events from my childhood. I have vivid memories of the houses we lived in and events that occurred when I was only a year and a half old. But I have one memory that I'm not sure is a memory at all. It's almost as though I'm in a scene. I'm in my bedroom in a white house, with a window overlooking an expansive field of green grass. I get out of bed and gaze out the window. The sky is clear blue. The grass is lush and green. White is the color of the house. Everything is beautiful. Everything is perfectly calm and peaceful.

In this scene, I know and feel that this is the perfect place. There is no stress. There is no ugliness. There isn't a single flaw. I have nothing to be sad about. It's not hot. It's not cold. The fact that I can feel it, long for it, that it's crystal clear, and it's where I want to go, leads me to believe that this is not a memory.

If I tell the kids at school, or even the kids at church, they might laugh at me. Perhaps this is a type of heaven or a representation of what heaven will look like. Perhaps this is how life should or will be for God's children. I've always heard that heaven is a perfect place, and the Bible confirms this.

Anyway, that's where I want to be right now, and it's where the notebook, "Images of Divine Things," takes me. Maybe that's why I'm thinking about it right now. The contrast between this wonderful location I envision and the insane stuff at school, like Doug, The Poop Artist with the rope around his neck, and all the locker room drama and other stressors... It seems like the difference between heaven and hell.

I tell Granddad about it, and as always, he gives me his whole attention.

"Granddad, I love that image notebook."

He breaks out in a wide smile. He merely nods his head and says nothing, but I know he's expressing that he knew I'd appreciate that book. I can see by his response that he enjoys it as well.

"Continue reading Bunyan and Edwards," he says.

THE ORCHARD

I T'S OCTOBER, AND THE TEXAS heat has given way to a brief
respite. I have nothing planned for Saturday. There's nothing
on at the movies that I want to see, and the lawn doesn't need
to be mowed. So, what will I do? The day is too beautiful to
stay inside, so I pack my books and head out to the orchard.

I flip through Edwards' journal. He includes entries about
trees as well as fruit. When he writes about trees, he is comparing them to God's Providence, or how God rules the earth
and directs all things. I've heard Granddad mention Providence,
but he's probably the only one I know who does. I don't recall
hearing that word anywhere else.

According to Granddad, Providence is God's rule over the
earth. He explains to me that God is the one who creates and
sustains everything. Granddad says it is mysterious and beyond
our comprehension.

"God's ways are higher than our ways," he says, "and the
Bible teaches that horrible things happen, but God may use
them to accomplish good."

I don't understand how good things can come from my parents' divorce, or how good things can come from me attending

a new school that I hate. I'm not sure how good can come from Doug and the terrors he inflicts on others. But the Bible, according to Granddad, teaches us that God can make man's wrath praise him.

I'm walking about the orchard, seeking for a spot where I can both lie down and sit up comfortably. I'm looking for a soft spot of grass to nap on once I finish reading. I also want a good back rest, so I am on the lookout for a comfortable tree. That is my goal for this Saturday. And I come across the perfect spot! I take a seat in front of the tree, lean against its trunk, raise my eyes, and gaze straight up through the branches. I can see the trees, the sky, and the fruit. It's an apple tree.

When I notice an apple within reach, I get up and pluck it. I take a big bite. It's amazing. I settle down again, and with Edwards in one hand and an apple in the other, I return to his musings on trees and Providence. He mentions twisting and turning as he depicts a tree and its numerous branches, as well as how they grow and their root system.

One thing I notice is that the trees lack any straight lines, and none of the apples are a perfect circle or sphere. When I glance around, I notice bees buzzing, flies flying, birds soaring through the air, and bugs crawling on the ground; everything appears to have order. I want my life to be smooth and straight, but there are always bumps in the road.

I'm thinking about Doug when I notice several dung beetles rolling a large ball of poop. I recall reading or hearing about the important role dung beetles play in eliminating animal feces from the ground. These insects, at least the ones I've seen, can be a beautiful metallic green or shiny black when they are rinsed off. Is Doug the human equivalent of a dung beetle? Is there a reason he's known as The Poop Artist? Could God have a plan for that and use it in some way? To do that, I believe God would have to be a very big God, which my granddad claimed he was. Could Doug be beautiful, even magnificent, if he was rinsed off? I don't think I'll ever look at Doug the same way again; either I'll see him as a dung beetle and The Poop Artist, or I'll think about how great he could be if he were just washed off. But one look at Doug and the trajectory of his life reveals that only God could cleanse him, because he is a mess.

I consider mean James. What type of insect is he? I'd have to think about it. What would he look like if he washed clean? What would stoners look like if they were cleaned up? How would the jocks appear if they were washed? How would the cowboys appear if they were washed thoroughly? I know God washed my sins away when I was much younger. I don't remember being that filthy. But, according to Granddad, the Bible teaches that both the young and the old need to be cleansed and saved through Christ. Every day, I feel as if I need to be washed.

I find myself praying more and more at Grandma and Granddad's house. I observe Granddad praying. In moments of isolation in the orchard, I see him rely on God for support and strength. He's old, and I'm sure he feels depressed at times.

Flipping through the books, I start reading a 1978 copy of *Garden History* with an article about Ralph Austen, an Oxford horticulturist and cider-maker from long ago. I see where Granddad wrote "Dialogue with Fruit Trees" in the margin of the article. As I read this article, I reflect on the insects around me, examine the tree I am resting on, taste its fruit, and gaze up at the sky. My thoughts begin to wander to faraway places.

I start to feel like I'm getting closer to that perfect place from my distant past. I picture what it's like to be there. To truly be present. And the perfect place is a real place where I can live. The more I think about it, the more I daydream about it, the heavier my eyelids become. A soft breeze touches my skin. The leaves rustle above and around me. I notice myself leaning while sitting on a soft patch of grass. I give in to the drowsiness and fall asleep.

———

Now I find myself in a different place, on a bed looking out a window. I realize I am now in the perfect place. In the distance, I see a lone tree in an open field. Suddenly I am near the tree and Granddad is there too. I can overhear Granddad having a conversation with the tree...

GRANDDAD: It's incredible to think that fruit trees can talk to us! Even though we can't hear them with our ears, they can still tell us things, answer our questions and give us helpful advice. What language do they use? Is it English, Latin, Greek, or Hebrew?

FRUIT TREE: We can understand and communicate with anyone in any language we come across! We can answer people in whatever speech they use to talk to us. Everyone can speak in their own tongue.

GRANDDAD: Let's talk in English since that's my native language. So, first of all, how old are the fruit trees in general? How long have they been around?

FRUIT TREE: We are from a very ancient time; even from the beginning of the world: which is now (according to what many people say) 6000 years or so: This you can understand by something that is very relevant to you; For we were there and watched when you and your wife both broke the command of our Creator, in the Garden of Eden, when you ate the Forbidden

Fruit: You were given plenty of freedom, which was to eat any of our fruits throughout the whole Garden; (except only one tree, to test your obedience) and you could do so as much as you wanted; so why did you disobey the command of God; which we have never done and never will, even though we are much less powerful than humans.

GRANDDAD: Here you can see the truth, and we must give thanks to God for it. We messed up horribly and lost our glory and joy, but God showed us a way to get back what we had before. He didn't do the same for the angels who sinned, but he showed us mercy and grace. We are now in a state where we can never fall again, and this is something that is revealed to us through the gospel of Christ. You don't really understand it, and you can't really explain it.

———

GRANDDAD: People have said that plants, trees, and other vegetation have a kind of connection between them - some kinds don't do well when they're together, and it's called 'antipathy', while other kinds do really well when they're together, and it's called 'sympathy'. What do you think about that?

FRUIT TREE: We understand the idea that different plants have different qualities and that some can thrive together, while others cannot. It's been said that there is an 'antipathy' between some plants, like the vine and the collard, but that's not true. Instead, it's because they both need the same soil and nutrients, and so they compete for them. However, there is an actual 'antipathy' between certain trees of different species, so they won't grow together when grafted. For example, an apple tree grafted onto a pear tree, or a plum onto a cherry tree. They may survive for a few years, but they won't thrive. So, it's important to make sure the right species and kinds are grafted together, or else there won't be any benefit for the gardener.

GRANDDAD: It's obvious that men and women have different ways of doing things, which can lead to tensions. But the biggest difference is between God, who is holy, and mankind, who is sinful. To be able to be near God and experience His presence, we must change our nature. We need to be transformed in our spirits and be given a new nature, through being united with Christ, so that we can look like the second Adam, who is pure and holy.

FRUIT TREE: So there can be no true friendship, happiness or joy between those who have been born again and those who have not, due to the opposition of their natures. What kind of relationship can Christ have with Satan, or a believer with an unbeliever? Thus, when it comes to choosing a spouse, it is best to make sure of this first and foremost, and all other considerations should come after.

GRANDDAD: Why should this be the case for fruit trees since you are not conscious beings and are lower in rank than them?

FRUIT TREE: We are not conscious creatures, but we are living beings with an innate sense of what is beneficial and detrimental to us. In warmer, more fertile soils, we thrive more than in cold, damp, barren locations. And so, depending on our position in relation to the sun, we choose to stay in the shade or bask in the light.

GRANDDAD: I can see that there is a great disparity among the creatures of this world, which can be broken down into four main groups. The first and lowest group consists of inanimate objects such as earth, water, stones, and minerals. The second group is a step up, consisting of living things such as plants and trees. The third group is even higher, composed of animals with senses. Lastly, the fourth group is the highest, made up of humans with the ability to reason.

GRANDDAD: Now, through the wisdom, providence, and design of God, creatures are distinct in their levels, with each level being more useful and helpful to the one above it. The simplest substances such as earth and water provide nourishment to the flowers, herbs, and all vegetation, and these in turn nourish the beasts, birds, fish, and so on. Finally, the highest rank of visible creatures, humans, are fed and nourished by all these so that they may serve and glorify God through them all.

———

GRANDDAD: I have spent a lot of time and energy on these fruit trees, digging around their roots and fertilizing the soil. I have also pruned the branches, cutting off half of them since they were too close and too many. I have also cut off half of the tree's height, as it had grown too tall and was vulnerable to the wind and frost. I hope all my hard work hasn't been in vain, so do you feel any better for all the time and effort I've put in?

FRUIT TREE: We feel like we're growing more strongly than ever before; we were held back by a tough outer layer that kept us from getting the nutrients we needed from the ground. But now, thanks to your help, that layer has been removed and we're getting plenty of nourishment. Our branches are no longer reaching for the sky, but instead they are spreading out and bearing lots of good fruit. We are so much better off thanks to your hard work.

GRANDDAD: I see it is as you say; Just like a wise and caring gardener, God takes care of His people, His spiritual fruit trees, and prunes them in special ways to help them produce more and better fruit.

GRANDDAD: For some Christians, once they have acquired a certain level of spiritual gifts and graces, they can become negligent and prideful, losing the vigor, zeal, and love they once had. As such, God acts as a husbandman, pruning away their excessive vanity, carnal thoughts and desires, and humbling them with afflictions and troubles, both physical and spiritual. In some cases, He will even withdraw His Spirit and allow them to fall into sin, as a way of curing their pride and self-love. Augustine once said that it is sometimes beneficial for a proud person to fall into a scandalous sin, in order to be humbled. He did not mean that it should be someone's choice to sin in order to be humbled, but that it is sometimes God's way of curing them.

GRANDDAD: A wise doctor can mix together medications in a way that can result in improved health. It is clear that God is in control of what we experience and should be praised and appreciated for it. We must learn from the struggles we face and be more grateful and productive in our lives afterwards.

———

GRANDDAD: It is an absolute pleasure to be here amongst all of you beautiful fruit trees! Seeing you all grow so strong and uniform is a sight to behold. Everywhere you look, you can see the perfect order and structure of everything. It's almost like a symphony to the eyes! Not only that, but the beauty of the blossoms, leaves and fruits with their bright colors, smells and tastes is simply mesmerizing. It's a feast for the senses and a delight for the mind.

FRUIT TREE: We recognize that what you say is true; we are indeed beautiful, desirable, and useful objects in the lives of men. However, you and others must be careful not to become too attached to us, for just like a serpent can hide amongst pleasant and beautiful flowers, the old serpent is still alive and can strike and harm you. Remember what happened in the Garden of Eden when your first parents were seduced by the beauty and excellence of the fruit they saw. They saw that the fruit was pleasing to the eye and good for food, so they ate it, being deceived by the cunning of the serpent. Rest assured that he has not lost any of his malice, power, or cunning, and is always on the lookout to do you and others harm.

GRANDDAD: This is a wise warning to take heed of and live by every day, for it is all too easy to let the things of this world overtake our devotion and love for God, leading to punishment and affliction from His hand. However, it is still possible to enjoy the creatures in moderation, and to use them as a reminder of the great mystery and privilege of being a believer: the ability to have communion and fellowship with God. True and humble Christians know from experience what it is like to walk with God in fellowship, and He graciously condescends to commune with those He has chosen, changed, sanctified, and prepared as vessels of mercy for His own use.

GRANDDAD: We don't have to hold back our love and affection as we should for the things of this world, since they are nothing compared to the infinite goodness of God. All the good and desirable things in the world are just a few drops coming from his infinite ocean. Being in God's presence is the ultimate joy and there are pleasures that last forever at his right hand.

———

GRANDDAD: People have long talked about the profits and joys that come from having orchards and gardens. Everyone usually praises the work of planting fruit trees due to the profits and benefits they bring. In addition to that, there are many added pleasures. So, what kind of profits and joys can we expect from fruit trees? Can you tell us some of the specifics?

FRUIT TREE: You understand that our fruits are incredibly beneficial and advantageous to people in many ways. They can be eaten and drunk throughout the year. It was the first food given to humankind in their most perfect state, even in Paradise, the most beautiful place on Earth. Our fruits were his designated sustenance, he could consume all of our fruits, except for one. And since then, fruits from trees have been a human's food and will continue to be until the end of time.

GRANDDAD: It's clear that the fruits of trees are an excellent source of nutrition for both humans and animals, especially when they're ripe. Cider is widely recognized as the healthiest drink available, and it's been supported by many learned and knowledgeable physicians. This has been proven by multiple generations in various countries, where it's used as a regular drink. In recent years, it's been praised by many esteemed people for its ability to promote health and longevity, something that's highly valued by all.

GRANDDAD: I believe that planting fruit trees is an incredibly beneficial and rewarding activity. Many have given it high praise and commendation, and I urge my fellow peers to get involved and reap the rewards of this activity. Not only will they benefit from it, but future generations will too.

GRANDDAD: The most important part of keeping an orchard is to think about the kind of trees you want to plant and make sure they have the right soil and position to get the most sunlight possible. There will be lots of benefits and joy in the end when you can eat the fruit you've grown and share it with your friends. It's so great to be able to enjoy and give away something you planted with your own hands!

GRANDDAD: People have said that the rewards of planting fruit trees are amazing and cannot be accurately calculated; the benefits are endless.

GRANDDAD: Augustine views this as a great activity, and one that is worthy of respect from the most talented people; as it has many hidden mysteries and secrets of nature that can be explored and studied by the most brilliant minds. Examining the nature of seeds planted, grafting twigs, and transplanting trees, are all activities that can be done to understand these phenomena, and then apply that knowledge accordingly. Ultimately, however, it is to be understood that it is not the planter or the waterer that brings about the growth, but God who is responsible for the increase.

GRANDDAD: Some theologians suggest that vineyards, gardens, orchards, and other enclosed areas are the Earth's heavenly havens and paradises.

GRANDDAD: Francis Bacon said that gardens are the most enjoyable activity for humans, providing a much-needed break from the monotony of buildings and palaces. They're a great way to revive the human spirit!

———

GRANDDAD: It's pretty obvious that planting fruit trees is both profitable and enjoyable, yet there are still a lot of people who don't do it. Why is this? A lot of young folks with land could really benefit from planting, but they're just not doing it. What could be the issue here? Is there something that's stopping them or discouraging them from getting started?

FRUIT TREE: At times it can seem disheartening to some people that the rewards of our efforts may not come quickly. We need to be patient and wait a few years before we can reap the benefits of our hard work. People who are focused only on immediate gratification and pleasure won't have the patience to wait for us to grow and produce plentiful results.

FRUIT TREE: Similarly, it appears that the effort and labor of planting trees is seen by many young, proud people as a lowly task, something that is too manual for them to be involved in. This attitude often prevents them from taking part in this incredibly beneficial activity.

GRANDDAD: It is clear that some young people with money often prioritize immediate pleasure over long-term gain, and are thus reluctant to invest in planting fruit trees, which require patience to yield a profit. However, more wise and mature individuals understand the great rewards that come with planting fruit trees and other kinds of trees, and are thus diligent in their efforts.

GRANDDAD: The pride of some people in thinking this work is beneath them and too manual is misguided. Just look at the work that God appointed to the first man in his state of happiness - to dress and keep the garden. There are many examples of great people who took great delight in planting fruit trees, including kings, emperors and other powerful figures - far from being ashamed of it, they performed it with their own hands. Emperor Dioclesian of Rome even left his empire to pursue this work in his later life. Others planted large and spacious orchards and used to feast and banquet with children and friends. King Cyrus of Persia, who had all the kingdoms of the Earth given to him, was diligent and exact in this work of planting fruit trees, doing it with his own hands.

GRANDDAD: People who think that tending to fruit trees is beneath them are mistaken; it's not just a few extraordinary people who have done it, but many, as evidenced by records from various authors. It's nothing to be ashamed of - no more than any other activity.

GRANDDAD: We should appreciate the value of planting fruit trees and the many advantages it offers. Not only does it provide us with temporal profits throughout our lives, but it also serves as a reminder to obey God's laws and follow the course of nature. Planting fruit trees is a work that carries the approval of all peoples.

GRANDDAD: Everybody agrees that two of the strongest arguments are those based on usefulness and those based on pleasure. Benefits and enjoyment are both convincing to people of all ages.

GRANDDAD: Pleasure is the salt of life, making it more enjoyable. The benefits of it are greater when it's combined with profit, and the pleasure is more intense when it's accompanied by rewards. Together, they create something that's better than either one alone.

———

GRANDDAD: I'm expecting more from these trees than just their looks. They're grown in a rich and fertile soil, so I'm not content with the meager returns they're giving me. I want more fruit and better profits than what I'd get from smaller trees growing in a poor soil.

FRUIT TREE: We should think about why our lack of fruitfulness might be due to our overindulgence in this rich, fertile soil. We know that being too full can be detrimental to reproduction in all living things. People who are overfed and become too large and plump rarely bear fruit, while those who are more moderate and temperate in their eating habits tend to have more success. This could be our situation, as our overfeeding in this deep and fertile soil causes us to grow big and produce a lot of shoots and broad leaves, but not much fruit.

GRANDDAD: It is clear to see that many of the great and powerful people of this world are living a life that is focused on temporal gains, while neglecting their spiritual wellbeing. They are living a life of pleasure and luxury, without considering the eternal consequences that come with it. It is foolish to choose a short-lived life of pleasure over the joy and glory of eternal life. Those who forget God should take this warning to heart, or else they will soon experience the terrible consequences of their neglect.

GRANDDAD: Yet I see a few of these grand trees even in this fertile soil, who, thanks to the skill and hard work of the farmer, produce excellent fruits in abundance every year. I would be overjoyed if all of you were so bountiful; I would then receive greater profits annually than I do now.

FRUIT TREE: You know from experience that too much of anything can be harmful and dangerous. So when you know the cause of a problem, it's best to get rid of it if you can, so the effect will go away too. This applies to both natural and moral or spiritual things.

GRANDDAD: This is helpful for those who are striving to be the best they can be, and for those who want to reach their highest potential.

GRANDDAD: Although the great wealth, titles, honors, riches, and pleasures of the world can be very tempting to those who possess them, the power of the Holy Spirit can still work in those people's lives to enlighten and change their minds and hearts from a state of nature to a state of grace. These people become famous examples to those around them, and they act as patterns of piety, charity, and virtue. They are truly noble, as they are born from above, and are sons and daughters of the Lord God Almighty. Unfortunately, most of these people still choose to walk on the broad path and enter through the wide gate that leads to destruction, as their minds are blinded by the glitter and splendor of the world's temptations. Yet, it is an incredible show of grace that some of them are chosen and called to be saved from the wrath to come, and are given an inheritance in heaven that will never fade away. Therefore, those who have been saved by God's grace should be filled with duty and thankfulness, and strive to obey Him.

————

GRANDDAD: I think you're feeling pretty confident and bold today, with your colorful flowers and lush greenery. Where did you get all this courage from?

FRUIT TREE: It delights our generous Creator to give it to us; but it is up to you, and for the sake of humanity that you are part of, and all others to recognize it; And serve him, and express our appreciation for him with more enthusiasm: This is our language, and lesson to all people; which every individual among us, speaks out loud each day: He who made me, for you, made you for himself.

GRANDDAD: I've seen you wearing plain clothes sometimes during the year. It looks like you switch up your outfit every now and then. Do you have a lot of different outfits?

FRUIT TREE: Yes, each year we are adorned with a new suit of clothing. Our generous Lord and Master bestows upon us a vibrant and fresh garment each spring. We look beautiful and full of life, surrounded by colorful flowers, leaves, and fruits. But as autumn approaches, the sun, the source of our life and growth, moves south and the vibrant clothing fades and falls off little by little until we are left bare and in a state of sorrow.

GRANDDAD: The ever-changing nature of life is something that we must all come to terms with - from wealth to poverty, health to sickness, honor to disgrace, good and bad reports - it's a rollercoaster of ups and downs that we have to be prepared for. To stay content in every situation, we must have a strong trust in God's love, which never changes and never wavers, no matter what life throws at us.

GRANDDAD: There's a big difference between summer and winter, but how do you manage during the cold winter months? Do you have any relief or sustenance to get you through the frost, snow, hail, rain, strong winds, and sometimes even destructive winds? You don't show any signs of life, like buds, blossoms, or leaves. How do you survive during these tough times?

GRANDDAD: Fruit trees struggle during the cold winter months, enduring the pinch of frost and other hardships.

GRANDDAD: The arrival of spring brings new life to the fruit trees, bringing them back to life.

FRUIT TREE: It's obvious that there's a huge difference between summer and winter; we lose our beauty and decorations, leaving us feeling almost lifeless. Some people might even think we're actually dead, but really we have a hidden energy inside of us that keeps us alive. When spring comes around and the sun gets closer, we start to feel a bit better. Even though we don't have senses, we still have a way of perceiving things. This is shown when our buds start to plump up, blossoms come out, and leaves and shoots appear. As the sun gets even closer and its heat and influence become stronger, we become more and more refreshed and our buds turn into fruits. We continue to flourish and bear fruit all summer long.

GRANDDAD: At times, life can be hard and full of struggles, just like the state of a desolate soul. For Christians, it's especially true as God withdraws from them and allows many trials and tribulations to come their way. These can come in the form of afflictions, temptations, and crosses that affect their bodies, names, estates, and relations. It's like a long night of darkness where life and hope seem to be gone, and they can't find God no matter how hard they search. It's like a difficult season of drought in which the poor and needy are searching for water, but there's none to be found. They cry out to God, but He seems to not hear them.

GRANDDAD: The darkness of this time can feel like a death sentence, and the feeling of being without God can be compared to the torment of Hell. Many people go through difficult times during this season, but when the Sun of Righteousness rises again, it brings comfort and joy to those who are weary and distressed. It's like a sailor who was almost sure to perish in a storm, but is then brought to safety and rejoices in their deliverance. This joy is indescribable and brings peaceable fruits of righteousness for the rest of their life. It's like the trees after a long, cold winter when the warm spring and heat of summer come, and everything flourishes in its beauty and glory.

———

GRANDDAD: Some learned people have speculated that the sap in fruit trees goes down from the branches to the roots in the fall, causing the leaves and fruit to drop and the branches to stop growing. Many woodcutters and others believe this to be an unquestionable fact. What do you think about this?

FRUIT TREE: If learned people and others think that way, they should think again and look more closely into the reasons for their opinion. We reject the idea; there's no way for us to give up any of our sap. Nature is smarter than that, and won't give up any sap it has acquired. Our sap is our life; it's our food and we use it to grow bigger and produce blossoms, leaves, and fruits every summer. How have we become so big and strong (as you can see)? It's from the sap we've taken in, and then our bodies have digested and assimilated it. We would be happy to get more sap if we could, but we won't give any of it back to our roots. Our roots already have plenty of sap all year round, more than we branches do.

FRUIT TREE: The natural and innate property of our sap is always to ascend; there is an active, vegetative spirit within us that is light and like a flame, and its appetite is always upwards. We can never part with any of our sap, or we would fade and decay. Our substance would be diminished, and if we decreased any part of the year by the descending of sap, then what would become of us? It is clear that there is no such thing as descending sap in trees.

GRANDDAD: I'm convinced that there's no such thing in nature as sap descending in fruit trees, and I have many reasons for it beyond what's been said. Without a cause, no effect can exist, and there's no legitimate cause for this phenomenon in nature. Therefore, we can conclude that it doesn't exist. As for leaves falling off trees in autumn and roots being better then, which some attribute to sap descending, the cause is misidentified. There are easier explanations for these effects: the leaves fall off because the sap has done ascending, and the roots are best then because they don't receive sap, so they're fed first.

GRANDDAD: We can learn lessons and instructions for spiritual advantages from the knowledge of fruit trees. The spiritual nature of true Christians naturally aspires and ascends upwards towards Christ, while corrupt nature tends downwards towards the creatures. Through this, we can examine ourselves and determine what nature or principle dwells in us. The tree is known by its fruit, and the effects of a cause can be seen. Therefore, by understanding fruit trees, we can gain insight into our spiritual selves.

———

GRANDDAD: In a sizable nursery of fruit trees, some are just are starting to grow, some are a bit bigger, and there are others that are already quite big; and of all these, some are grafted, and some ungrafted. I think that the biggest and oldest trees should be transplanted and moved out of the nursery, to different places such as orchards, gardens, and fields; that way they can have room to grow and provide lots of good fruit for many people to benefit from.

FRUIT TREE: It's clear: Such big, beautiful trees should be taken away from the younger ones, so that we, the young, can have room to grow and thrive. Otherwise, these tall trees will cross and tangle with each other, and get in the way of one another. It's important that they be removed so that others can come up in their place and grow, eventually being taken away to somewhere where they can expand and bear fruit for years to come.

GRANDDAD: I understand that the ultimate goal of planting a nursery of fruit trees is to get them ready for transplanting elsewhere. However, it is also important to keep some of the best trees in the nursery in order to get grafts and fruit from them, so that the ungrafted trees can eventually be prepared for transplanting.

GRANDDAD: It's important for young people to understand that universities and learning societies are like nurseries for spiritual fruit trees. They are designed to prepare youth to be fruitful and glorify God. Everyone should work hard to be gifted and qualified with learning and other endowments of the mind. Those who have been given talents should use them for their master's use, so they can receive a reward. It's also essential that some of the chief and principal fruit trees remain in the nursery for governors and tutors to help the younger sort be prepared for different roles in the church and state.

GRANDDAD: Now, the most important thing to strive for and obtain is the Spirit and Grace of God. Natural abilities and learning, improved by study and hard work, are incredibly useful and beneficial, and all efforts should be used to attain them. But these alone are not enough to reach the highest goal - the glory of God. By nature, humans can have no higher purpose than themselves and their own interests. It's like water, which can only rise as high as its source. Everything acts according to its nature and can do no different. Thus, a divine principle is essential. This is, spiritually, the Philosopher's Stone, which turns all natural achievements into gold. It uses and improves everything for spiritual purposes and aims, in order to glorify

God. We must acquire this, or we get nothing. Everyone should be like Luther, who earnestly begged God to not give him merely worldly or natural gifts. We should be persistent with God and not accept a refusal. Even if we ask for temporal things conditionally (if it be the will of God to give them), we should ask for spiritual things (which are absolutely necessary) without condition. The Kingdom of Heaven is taken by force, and the violent will take it.

———

GRANDDAD: I see a lot of trees in this orchard that look really big and healthy, with broad green leaves and pretty flowers. But they don't produce any good fruit. The ones they do have are big and colorful, but they taste bad - sour and bitter. The orchard keeper doesn't like it. If they don't start producing better fruit soon, they'll be chopped down and used for firewood.

FRUIT TREE: We thrive in a fertile and healthy environment, and are as big and solid as any other trees, producing fruit in accordance with our kind. We have not been grafted like other trees, so we remain rooted in our natural, wild stock, thus producing fruit accordingly. This is likely to continue until we are grafted onto something new.

GRANDDAD: Here we see the likeness and similarity of those who pretend to be religious in the Church, but are not truly devoted to God. They may appear to be pious and devout, but they are not truly connected to Christ, and their actions are not done for the glory of God. Consequently, their deeds are not accepted by God, and they should take this time to ensure they have a genuine faith in Christ.

———

GRANDDAD: A bunch of mulberry trees are standing in a row, and they're obviously pretty important. People use the leaves to feed silkworms and make syrups with the fruit. In ancient times they were thought to be the wisest of trees. So, what's the reason for this? How do these trees get to be so wise? What do the trees have to say about themselves?

FRUIT TREE (MULBERRY): We do not possess the title of 'wise', as we are not more knowledgeable than other trees. However, some people may say this of us because we do not show our buds or blossom until the start of May, when the cold weather has passed. This is simply the way of nature and how we were created, and it is in this that the wisdom of our Creator is seen. We are of a more fragile and delicate nature than many other fruit trees, which may bud and blossom up to six weeks or two months before us. If we were to appear earlier, we would not be able to withstand it.

GRANDDAD: It is definitely clear that different kinds of fruit trees have different needs and characteristics, so they must be planted and looked after in the right way. Some are so delicate that they won't survive or bear fruit unless they are planted against a south-facing wall and looked after with great care. On the other hand, some can thrive and produce fruit even in open fields, despite cold temperatures, frost, storms, and wind.

GRANDDAD: In the same way, some Christians have a greater capacity to face and handle spiritual struggles than others. Some have a strong faith, while others have a much weaker faith. Some have a great measure of the Spirit of God, wisdom, and knowledge, while others are still in the early stages of understanding and grace. Some Christians have a deep love for Christ and strong zeal for him, while others have a much weaker love and can do little for him. The cause is weak, so the effects are the same.

———

GRANDDAD: I find it interesting that some types of fruit trees ripen their fruit gradually, with some parts of the same tree bearing ripe fruit weeks before the rest. Examples of this include apricots, peaches, cherries, and plums. Meanwhile, other types of trees ripen their fruit all at once, such as some apple trees, and all winter fruits. I'm curious as to why there is this difference in the ripening of fruits on trees.

FRUIT TREE: Behold the wisdom, generosity, and goodness of our Creator! If we cherry trees, plum trees, and other summer fruits, were to bear all of our fruits at once, there would be an abundance, and we would do more harm than good. For we are not long-lasting; we would soon rot in a few days. Therefore, God gives us our fruits one day at a time, so that you and others can make use of them for health and profit. As for hard winter fruits, they are ripe all at once, so they can be gathered and stored for use throughout the year. Is this not the same wisdom, generosity, and goodness from God, shown to all people in different ways, as has been said?

———

GRANDDAD: It's kind of strange that some trees don't seem to be doing as well as the others even though they're planted and taken care of the same way. What could be the cause of this?

FRUIT TREE (FOREIGN): We are outsiders; this is not our homeland as we were brought from across the oceans, from a warm climate; where we had a powerful heat, and the rays of the sun; however, we are now in a frigid land, and it does not suit us, we will never thrive, nor succeed, nor produce any fruits to bring you pleasure, or any benefit.

GRANDDAD: I agree that it is true that many well-off individuals have imported and planted plants and trees from countries in the south, such as France, Spain, and Italy, even though they are located further north. Although these plants can produce many kinds of fruits suitable for the climate, they will not bear oranges, lemons, pomegranates and other fruits of southern countries. Therefore, it is better to invest in fruit trees that have been proven to be profitable for those who plant them.

———

GRANDDAD: Here are Redstreak trees full of delicious apples: are these the same Redstreaks that make the renowned cider in Herefordshire, so popular among everyone? How did they become so sought after now? It hasn't been long since they were known as Skidmores Crabs; wasn't that a slight to the trees and fruits? How did they come to be so sought after and appreciated everywhere now?

FRUIT TREE: It's true; we've been around for quite a while, and our apples have been known as Skidmores Crabs, but they've been underrated for a long time. However, when people took the time to get to know us and try out our apples, they found that they make the best cider. Nowadays, we're highly praised and appreciated by everyone.

GRANDDAD: I am aware that life can be challenging and that it often happens that God's people may find themselves in difficult situations due to sin, temptations and afflictions. However, God in His own good time can bring them out of these troubles and restore them to a place of esteem and honor, greater than those who have not gone through the same. An example of this is the Prodigal Son, for when their true nature and fruit is revealed, God will bring them praise and fame in every place they have been shamed. Zephaniah 3:19.

———

GRANDDAD: Many have noticed that there has been a lot of planting of fruit trees in recent years, more than in the past. People have planted more fruit trees in the last 30 or 40 years than in hundreds of years previously, as evidenced by the orchards that have been planted. What is the reason that fruit trees are so popular now, more so than in the past?

FRUIT TREE: It is clear why people have become more interested in fruit trees recently; not only do they provide a profitable sale, but they also provide a delicious and nutritious food source all year round. Cider, in particular, is now widely accepted as the most healthful drink available, having been proven to both prevent and cure various illnesses. Therefore, it is no surprise that fruit trees are more highly valued than ever before.

GRANDDAD: It's clear that cider is the healthiest and most beneficial drink out there, made from everyday fruits. But there are some special fruits that make the cider even better than the ordinary kind, like Redstreak and Gennet Moyles. As long as people value health and longevity, cider will remain popular as a means to achieve these goals.

———

GRANDDAD: I totally understand that fruit trees are amazing creations of God that demonstrate his glory and wisdom. It's so clear to us that God is so powerful, good, generous, caring, and loving when we look at them. We should take them as examples and be inspired to be as obedient and devoted to God as they are. We should also strive to show God's glory even more than they do, since we are more advanced than them and were created for a higher purpose.

FRUIT TREE: Truly, you must strive to make the glory of the Almighty your highest priority, and act accordingly, for else we will one day testify against you. We are here to serve as examples, motivators, and encouragers for you to obey God.

GRANDDAD: At the end of it all, human beings are driven by their own self-interests and desires, and often put themselves before anything else. This is just a part of our natural inclination, and unless God works to instill a spiritual and divine nature in us, we will continue to act solely for our own benefit. However, with the Spirit's guidance, we can learn to put God's interests before our own and work for His glory.

FRUIT TREE: You are telling us of something mysterious, we do not recognize any such thing in ourselves; like a transformation in our characters; what do you mean by a transformation of character; we have never altered our personalities, from the start of time until now; and we have adhered to and respected the rules of our formation, without any breach; and we will continue to do so until the end of days.

GRANDDAD: It's no secret that humans have changed since the day we were first created. We've gone from a state of holiness to a state of sin and corruption due to our disobedience.

But there's another change that's happened to some of us, which you don't know about. It's the change from a state of sin and corruption to a state of grace and holiness. This is something that only some people experience, who are called and sanctified in their lifetime and eventually saved.

————

GRANDDAD: I've noticed that the trees that get the most sun produce the best fruits, while those that are in the shade don't seem to be nearly as good. What do you think is the reason for this difference in the fruits?

FRUIT TREE: The reason is clear and obvious: We who grow in the sun are greatly revitalized by its warmth and energy, it is the driving force behind our life and growth. In the spring, we can feel its approach, drawing closer and closer each day, and we are delighted by it; expressing this joy through our budding, blooming, and producing of fruit. Our fruits are also ripened and matured better by the heat of the sun than those that grow in the shadows.

GRANDDAD: It's clear that as Christians, we benefit from walking closely with God. The closer we get, the more fruitful and sweet our lives become. God is our sun and shield, providing us with refreshment and protection. Psalm 84:11 confirms this.

————

GRANDDAD: Here are many fruitful trees that yield abundant and nutritious fruits every year, providing us with great benefit. How long will they continue to bless us with their beauty, virtue, and profit?

FRUIT TREE: As we have been since the dawn of time; and we have been aiding the first human; so we shall stay until the end of the world; providing our service to the last person, The Bible states that fruit trees have been here since the start; and will remain until the end.

GRANDDAD: God created Adam and put him in the Garden of Eden. He caused all types of fruit trees to grow, and gave the fruit to Adam for food. The Bible also states that when Christ returns to judge the world, people will be planting and building, just like in the days of Noah. Luke 17:28 says that it will be the same when the Son of Man comes.

GRANDDAD: Where does all your excellent virtue come from; your good and helpful qualities that benefit people? What is the initial source, the starting point, of all your admirable qualities?

FRUIT TREE: Our generous and wise Creator gifted us with individual distinct characteristics and qualities, as it pleased Him.

GRANDDAD: It is clear that all the wonder and excellence in the world, in the sky, on the land, and in the sea, all the beauty, sweetness, and goodness, are all united in God, who is the ultimate good. From beholding his creations and making use of their virtues and properties, we should be drawn to God and prefer him above all else, recognizing him as the supreme good.

———

GRANDDAD: I observe a bunch of youthful, small trees that are bursting with beautiful, delectable, and delightful fruits, which is a very extraordinary sight. Despite only being three or four years old since being grafted, they are producing more fruit than other trees in the vicinity that are over 80 years old. What could be causing this?

FRUIT TREE: We were all of us nurtured while we were still young, and small saplings, with careful selection and special grafts, so it's natural for us to bear good fruit early on.

GRANDDAD: At God's pleasure, it is acceptable for Him to graft some when they are young, while leaving others to grow without it. Who can find fault with Him for exercising His freedom and liberty? Similarly, Christians are dealt with in different ways. Some God calls and converts early in their childhood and youth, while others come to Him in their middle age or later. Those who come to God in their youth have many advantages over those who come later. God commands that we come to Him early, as soon as possible in our youth. Those who choose to serve the devil and their own desires in their youth and think to come to God later should hearken to His warning that He will laugh at their calamity and mock them when their fear comes.

GRANDDAD: Those who begin to follow God in their childhood and youth, and bear good fruit during their tender years, usually know more of God's mind and love than others. We see examples of this in the Bible, such as Samuel the Prophet, Jeremiah, Joseph, Obadiah and Daniel. These people received remarkable favors from God, and Daniel even had an angel sent to him with a special message. Similarly, David was taught of God from his youth and had clear evidences of God's love and communion with Him.

GRANDDAD: John the Baptist was an incredible prophet, filled with the Holy Spirit and blessed from birth. The beloved disciple, John, began to follow Jesus in his youth and was particularly close to Him, leaning on His breast and lying in

His bosom. This closeness resulted in a deep assurance of God's love for him. Those who are grafted into Christ while they are young can grow in grace and measure if they start with a small seed of faith. Every act of grace will add to the habit of grace, and they will go from strength to strength, and from glory to glory, guided by the Spirit of the Lord.

———

GRANDDAD: You've had a lot of guests coming through, and do you have the same kind of conversations with each one as we are having right now, as often as we feel like it?

FRUIT TREE: Many people come and go, taking in the sight of our grandeur and beauty, especially when we are in full bloom, with our vibrant blossoms and delicious, nutritious fruit. Some of them even greedily pluck us and tear us, snatching away our fruit and leaving without a word. But we never tire of speaking to them, trying to teach them about their duty to our Creator and praising and extolling His glory, as is our purpose and what we were made for. You have seen this many times, and it is our mission to continue to do so.

GRANDDAD: I think it's safe to say that most people in the world don't really have a clue about God, themselves, and all the things He created. Even though God gave us two amazing books, His Word and His works, most people don't really take the time to read and understand them. The prophet calls them sottish children, meaning they lack understanding and won't be shown mercy or favor by the one who made them, Isa 27:11.

GRANDDAD: Be amazed by this proclamation, you foolish and ignorant people; there will be no compassion for you, while you stay oblivious to God, yourself, His words, and His works. Therefore, study and be educated, or else you will surely be destroyed; even the plants of the garden and all of God's creations will testify against you.

GRANDDAD: The illiterate person who can't read a single word or letter in the book may think they can get away with it, but they'll soon find out that's not true. This book of God's creatures is open and understandable to everyone. As Paul said in Romans 1, those who don't learn from it will be left without excuse. We need to pay attention to the voices of the creatures of God, including the fruit trees, as well as the words of God. When we put the two together, we can understand what God wants of us and be blessed by him.

———

GRANDDAD: Let us now venture forth into this delightful garden, and have a conversation with the gentle, harmless fruit trees. They will greet us warmly and are always willing to chat with us, always teaching us something valuable. But we must not forget that their discourse is not heard with our physical ears, but with our inner senses, our minds and hearts. They will talk to us for as long as we want and always speak in a wise and reverent way, praising God and giving us guidance for both our physical and spiritual well-being.

GRANDDAD: This large garden is a sight to behold, with its lush greenery and abundant fruit trees, providing both benefit and enjoyment. I've heard there are many things here that can leave people in awe - what are they? Let's hear what you have to say about yourselves!

FRUIT TREE: You can marvel at the wondrous wisdom, strength, and goodness of God when you consider our beginnings. We were all wrapped up in tiny seeds, each no bigger than a grain of wheat, yet these huge and vast bodies have sprung forth from them. Every seed stays true to its own kind and nature, even though many sorts are planted in a single patch of earth and draw the same nourishment from the soil.

FRUIT TREE: And secondly: If you take a look at how our fruits come into being (especially those of the most delicate varieties, like apricots, cherries, and plums), you can see that they come with a protective coating or garment on them, which is necessary for them to survive in the open air. When the time is right, you can observe the little fruit inside the blossom, no bigger than a pinhead, gradually growing and tearing away its protective covering until it is strong enough to endure the air and reach full ripeness.

FRUIT TREE: But those of us who are stronger and hardier, like apples, pears and other fruits, don't have any kind of covering when we're born. We're completely bare when we enter the world and our blossoms fall away when we start to form. Then, we grow until we reach perfection.

GRANDDAD: I understand then that what some wise philosophers refer to as the wisdom of nature, in looking after itself, is actually the law of nature, and the wisdom of the divine Creator. Since he is the one who made all creatures, he knows their individual characteristics and provides for them accordingly.

———

GRANDDAD: This is impressive to say the least; What else can you tell us about it?

FRUIT TREE: Behold and ponder the marvels of nature! Can you not be awed by the fact that so many different things can be created from one single substance? From the sap of trees, we can make bark, wood, pith, leaves, buds, blossoms, stalks, fruit, and seed, all derived from the same nourishment of the earth.

FRUIT TREE: This shows us that in spiritual matters, the same applies; the variety of gifts and blessings given to believers come from the same Spirit. As it says in 1 Corinthians 12:4, there are various gifts, but it is the same Spirit that gives them; and there are various ways of serving, but it is the same Lord; and verse 6 says there are various kinds of operations, but it is the same God who works in all. To some is given the word of wisdom, to another the word of knowledge; to someone the gifts of healing, to another the ability to perform miracles; to another prophecy; to another the ability to discern spirits; to another various kinds of tongues; and to another the ability to interpret tongues.

FRUIT TREE: Yet all these are empowered by the same spirit, who gives out their gifts as he pleases: 1 Cor. 12:12.

FRUIT TREE: We should strive to learn to appreciate and care for one another, regardless of our individual gifts and talents. We should not let the wealthy look down on the poor, nor should the poor be envious of the wealthy. We should not let the wise and educated scorn the less fortunate who may lack what they have. Everyone has something to offer, and no part of the body is more important than another. We should remember that even the seemingly weaker parts of the body are essential.

FRUIT TREE: The many talents and abilities that people have are all gifts from the same source, and should be used to bring honor and benefit to all.

GRANDDAD: Go on, tell us more of the amazing, awe-inspiring works of God. So many wonders of His creation surpass our understanding, so let us take the time to marvel in the glory of God and His wondrous works.

FRUIT TREE: Contemplate this further: Grafts and buds placed on wild, sour and bitter stocks can still develop a sweet and pleasant nature, transforming the sour sap they draw and feed on into their own properties. The badness of the stocks cannot change the goodness of the grafts, as all vegetation follows the law and course of nature, converting all the nourishment they take into their own properties and producing fruit accordingly.

FRUIT TREE: It is truly amazing that such a vast and mighty force (it could be 40 times larger than the graft that is placed upon it) cannot change a smaller graft or bud into its own kind. This can only be attributed to the innate, intrinsic form of the graft and bud that preserves and upholds the law of nature that the Creator established at the beginning of creation. All praise and admiration is due to Him for these and all of His works.

———

GRANDDAD: What else do you find in the process of Nature that showcases God's wisdom and greatness and is worthy of admiration and praise once it is understood?

FRUIT TREE: Realize and consider this further: Every small branch or twig on the trees, even the slightest bud on the tiniest graft or twig, holds within it the nature and characteristics of the entire tree. Even though one tree may have thousands of buds, each one has all the potential of the whole tree, no matter how small the bud or how big the tree. This is clear when you inoculate the buds of any tree - consistent experience demonstrates that they will produce the same fruits as the tree they were taken from.

GRANDDAD: It's wonderful to think that something as small as a grain of wheat or even smaller can contain all the properties of a huge tree. Experience has proven that if the small root of a bud is left behind when trying to inoculate, the bud won't grow at all. That's why those who take on this task of inoculating have to make sure the small root is included when it is set on the stock. It's truly incredible that such a tiny part of a tree can be so important for it to be able to grow.

GRANDDAD: The same seeds from the same tree can produce different kinds of fruit! It's like each seed holds the potential for a variety of different kinds of apples, pears, or whatever kind of tree it came from. It's incredible that even though the seeds are all the same, the fruit they produce can be so different.

GRANDDAD: It's amazing how God's generosity shines through in the diversity of plants! From the same seed, we can get different types of flowers, some double, some single, some one color, some another. We should be in awe of this and give thanks to God for providing us with such a variety of wonderful creatures, both for pleasure and for necessity. Let's show our gratitude by living more cheerfully and taking full advantage of all the benefits we receive.

––––––

GRANDDAD: There's so much to be amazed by in nature! Every year, we have the opportunity to witness the beauty of the Creator's work. We should take the time to appreciate and marvel at the wonders of the Lord. His work is honorable and glorious, and we should come and behold it for ourselves.

God has done such incredible things that they deserve to be remembered and celebrated.

FRUIT TREE: We find many things to be observed and celebrated by everyone; the everlasting might, intellect, kindness, and generosity of God is evident in us, in addition to what has been expressed or can be said, take note of this further.

FRUIT TREE: At the base of one great apple tree, a variety of different kinds of apples can be grafted, if desired. Depending on the number of branches, there could be 20, 30, 40, or more different kinds of apples. Some may be early-ripening, some late, some large, some small, but they all grow on the same tree and feed from the same sap. Yet, each graft will produce its own unique fruit.

GRANDDAD: I have seen a variety of fruits on one tree, and it's possible that many more kinds could have been grafted onto it if people wanted to. These different grafts yielded different fruits, each one producing its own kind. This proves the assertion of a wise philosopher to be true - grafts have control, all grafts govern, even when they're grafted onto a different stem. They take the different sap they feed on and transform it into their own nature, and the fruits they produce reflect this.

GRANDDAD: This idea could be useful for both financial gain and enjoyment; someone with a small plot of land for their orchard can still have a variety of fruits from a few trees; depending on the size and breadth of the trees, they can expand their grafts with whatever types they think are best.

———

FRUIT TREE: You have asked us many questions, and we have reflected at length on the wisdom and message of fruit trees. Do you mind if I ask you some questions about your perception of revelation in God's creation?

GRANDDAD: Certainly! I welcome any questions from you that will further our conversation.

FRUIT TREE: I am but one volume in the huge series of the Book of Nature. And though I have seen much, I would like to hear about the other books. Surely our discussion has stimulated your reflection on the other aspects of God's creation.

GRANDDAD: You are right. It seems like thousands of connections have lit up in my mind when I think about how God has spoken through his Word and his works. It is as if he has provided humans a unified revelation, a single book that has pictures along with text.

FRUIT TREE: Can you explain this unified revelation further?

GRANDDAD: The pictures are shadows of divine things and the Scriptures have a close connection. By taking time to reflect, we can understand the divine message that is being represented in the world around us. God speaks to us through these symbols and verifies the teachings of the Bible. The world is filled with signs and symbols that point to spiritual reality. For instance, vines, light, and bread represent Christ, while milk symbolizes the Word of God. God uses the events in our lives to reveal His will. We must be careful not to let our imaginations get away from us, and we must always interpret and apply the Scriptures to the emblems we see. The physical world was made to show us spiritual truth, and the ancients saw all things in the world as signs and shadows of the spiritual realm. God loves to teach us through His works, and we should be open to discovering the messages He has for us.

———

FRUIT TREE: It makes perfect sense that God, who is so wise, would use his creations to speak to intelligent beings and reveal divine mysteries. His works are like a language, teaching the attentive about Him and His spiritual kingdom. It's no surprise that He loves to use this method of instruction, since we know He takes great joy in it.

GRANDDAD: If we want to get a better understanding of the world around us, it's important to view it with an attitude of faith. Wearing the "spectacles" of faith allows us to explore a much bigger and more meaningful perspective.

———

FRUIT TREE: Do the works of God have anything to say of his fatherly love?

GRANDDAD: The doctrine of revelation teaches that a kind God reveals himself through all that is around us. From the sky to the fields, from the blessings we receive to the medical knowledge we have, all of it is a reflection of the Father's and Creator's love. The storm shows us his power and anger, while the rainbow and the blooming fields after a shower show us his tenderness and loving kindness. Rivers, with their winding course and nourishment, represent his providence and care. The sun, with its light and heat, is a symbol of God's faithfulness and love. But the deep places, along with thunder and lightning, ocean storms, and river cataracts, all show us his wrath and the horrible torments of hell. All of these things demonstrate our dependence on God, and should make us consider the grandeur of the universe and the infinite nature of God.

———

GRANDDAD: It should be stressed that the "spectacles of faith" do not make use of philosophical or scientific means. Even though these methods may be helpful, they don't give us the full picture of what the Creator had in mind. The language of God's works is understood through immediate impressions, followed by reflection and meditation which reveals their correlation with Scripture.

FRUIT TREE: This is all very good, since fruit trees are not philosophers! We are deeply interested in how the wider world reveals God.

GRANDDAD: Though one does not need to be a philosopher, having a keen appreciation for poetry is a great help, and even a requirement. God is an artist and poet. The natural world is a reflection of God's method of working in similitudes, and thus is an indication of spiritual reality. The universe Is a huge cathedral of spiritual symbols, with stars, planets, and the sun and moon representing the saints, angels, and Christ in Heaven. The insignificance of the world in comparison to the vastness of space shows the smallness of worldly grandeur in comparison to the glory of Heaven. The physical world points to the spiritual world, and that miracles like the parting of the Red Sea and the sun standing still during Joshua's time were proof of this. Ecclesiastes 1:7 to illustrates the idea that worldly pursuits are ultimately futile, as the river never stops flowing to the sea. Nature's types can only be correctly understood in the light of Scripture, as it holds the spiritual truths that the illustrations are based on.

FRUIT TREE: Trees have witnessed almost every facet of God's creation, even the depths of the ocean. During the great flood in the time of Noah, while submerged, we saw Leviathan and other monsters. Though we had done nothing wrong, we experienced the terrors of the deep. Please, go on!

———

GRANDDAD: It is helpful to understand that the great cathedral of creation is divided into several categories or realms. The sky is the first realm of creation, the highest on the scale of existence. It contains elements such as light, stars, the highest of heavens, the visible heavens, the sun, moon, planets, comets, the rainbow, atmospheric events, and night.

GRANDDAD: The Earth and Waters are the second realm, which includes rivers, springs, wells, seas, waves, rain, floods, cataracts, fish, mountains, hills, valleys, caverns, volcanoes, fire and brimstone, dirt, precious metals, and jewels.

FRUIT TREE: I have seen power of God is reflected in the raging seas and rivers in a storm, a representation of His terrible wrath and the misery of those who have to endure it.

GRANDDAD: The Bible often uses water to symbolize misery of being overwhelmed, such as in Psalms 88:7 and 42:7. Job 27:20 states, "Terrors take hold as waters," and Hosea 5:10 says, "I will pour out my wrath upon them like water." Psalms 42:7 goes even further, comparing God's wrath to cataracts of water: "Deep calleth unto deep at the noise of thy waterspouts." Additionally, the same is represented in hail, stormy winds, dark clouds, and thunder.

GRANDDAD: As a fruit tree, you are intimately aware of the third realm which consists of trees, plants, flowers, fruits, grains, their life cycles and usefulness or uselessness, and the effort needed to cultivate and harvest them.

FRUIT TREE: Yes, I am well versed in all facets of the life of trees and plants, as you can see from our earlier conversations.

GRANDDAD: The fourth realm is Birds which nest in your branches. This includes doves, crowing roosters, young birds and their mothers, singing birds, ravens, crows, eagles, vultures, and owls.

GRANDDAD: Animals are the fifth realm, and include sheep, milk, wool, skins, conception, embryos, miracles, lions, tigers, crocodiles, foxes, cats, mice, serpents, swine, whales, dragons, and all venomous and predatory animals.

GRANDDAD: Insects are the sixth realm, which includes bees, silkworms, grasshoppers, flies, spiders, and all other insects.

FRUIT TREE: Ah yes, the bees who pollinate our blossoms! We need the assistance of the honey bee. Without them, many apple trees would not be able to yield any apples. The pollen from the blossoms of a tree can't pollinate its own flowers. Bees are needed to move the pollen from one tree to another, allowing the production of fruit. Bees and apple trees are connected in a strong relationship. We are mutually beneficial to each other and our collaboration helps us to make delicious fruit!

GRANDDAD: And the seventh realm is Man, which includes his breath, blood, body, heart, tongue, tears, head, posture, love, marriage, birth, children, parenting, government, celebrations, games, judgment, names, sleep, garments, nakedness, bowels, inwards, excrement, death, putrefaction, dirt, corpse, and embalming. Man-made things and activities, which are quite diverse and complex, comprise an eighth realm.

———

FRUIT TREE: I can see that the revelation of God in his works stretches from the highest heavens to the lowest depths. Emblems of his glory are inscribed over all of his creation!

GRANDDAD: You are right. Rivers and streams are symbols of God's providence, his government of the entire creation. Even though at time rivers and streams may seem to flow away from the sea, or in contrary directions, they are actually all connected and arrive at a common destination. The same concept can be seen in machines and gears, like a clock with different wheels and gears turning at different speeds and in different directions, yet they still work together to achieve the goal of moving the hands to tell time. Rivers and machines both represent God's providence and although it may seem like obstacles or contrary movements hinder the advancement of his kingdom, it will all come together to fulfill his plan and glorify him. Even everyday activities and things, such as farm animals, illustrate divine purpose. Horses carry riders, cows produce milk and sheep wool, and pigs are a symbol of rebellious people who do not carry God's image. All of these things can be seen as examples of God's providence and purpose.

GRANDDAD: The stars in the sky are said to have mysterious influence over the world and its people, revealing how God administers providence through supernatural beings, both good and bad. God questions Job, asking if he can control the stars and their constellations, and if he knows the laws of the heavens. Snakes and spiders are also symbols of the devil, since they sneak up on their prey and inject their venom. Flies are thought to represent the evil spirits and wicked men, and the prince of the devils is called "Baalzebub," which means "lord of the flies." Owls and other night creatures represent devils, and their cries are the cries of those condemned to eternal darkness. Animals like cats, lions, tigers, and crocodiles are also linked to Satan, as they instill fear in the defenseless. The serpent in Genesis 3:14 has a curse placed on it, which symbolizes the curse placed on Satan.

FRUIT TREE: I too have seen these representations of the enemy. Ravens and crows do not feast on the remains of creatures until they are no longer living; thus, the devil does not take the souls of wicked people into his punishing grasp and ravenous mouth until they have passed away. In this way, the corpse, being dead and decaying, is a vivid representation of a soul in the wretched state it is in under everlasting death.

———

GRANDDAD: In Malachi, the sun's light is a symbol of Christ's power and influence in the heavens. The sun's beams are not able to be disrupted by the most powerful winds on earth, which is a representation of the eternal light and comfort that comes from Christ. The sun is so pure and high up that the winds can't touch it, and this is comparable to how Christ's power is not affected by the storms and changes of this life. The sun's rising signifies the end of the Jewish law and the beginning of the Gospel. It also symbolizes the Son of Righteousness coming to judge those who reject Him. The union of Adam and Eve is an emblem of Christ and his church, and the authority of the head over the body is similar to how Christ has authority over his spiritual body. When Christ died, the sun lost its light, and when he rose, the sun rose with him. Plants, insects, animals, and birds all have ties to Christ's benevolence - a tree and its branches represent Jesus and his church, and a bird on its nest symbolize Christ caring for believers. All of these things show how Christ's incarnation, atonement, and inheritance are represented in the world. The red sunset is a sign of Christ's blood, ripe red fruit depicts his blood, and sheep being sheared is a representation of Christ's work in providing believers with garments of righteousness. Lastly, the way wheat is beaten to make bread and grapes are crushed to make wine are both symbols of the agony Christ endured in order to save us.

FRUIT TREE: I have observed an image of Christ in the labor of the silkworm which produces silk. This symbolizes Christ's sacrifice. The silkworm works diligently, sacrificing its life in the process, and in its death, it completes the task of creating something beautiful for us to wear. It is then resurrected, a glorified creature, just as Christ was in His resurrection. The silkworm leaves behind its web of white silk, signifying the purity of grace that Jesus was given when He rose from the dead. This garment is a reminder of the righteousness of the saints.

———

GRANDDAD: Along with Christ, emblems of the Holy Spirit are found throughout the world. The colors of a rainbow, the whiteness of all colors combined, and the breath of life all represent the Spirit. The relationship between the Spirit and believers are like a bird and her young. The bird shelters them, brings them forth, and feeds them, just as the Spirit shelters, brings forth, and nourishes the souls of believers. There is a connection between the Spirit and revival, comparing it to the creation of the world from a dark and chaotic deep, the rekindling of a nearly extinguished fire, and a rain shower on a parched land. Ezekiel 37:9-14 and John 20:22 further illustrates this point.

————

GRANDDAD: Humans, with their upright posture and behavior, provide a variety of emblems. One of the most obvious is that humans were made in the image of God. This is in contrast to other animals, whose heads are pointed down at the ground. This emphasizes that humans can only find true fulfillment in heaven, not on earth like the rest of the creatures. Another example is that, like the old coins with Caesar's image, God has put His image on people and claims them as His own. This means that humans and the lower creation share many features. Good people can be likened to fruitful trees, while wicked people are only useful as fuel. Life is like a flame or mist - it can be easily snuffed out by a small gust of air. This is emblematic of how fragile life is. Furthermore, the names of people in the Bible often represent their personalities, and the natural world can be used to show spiritual reality. For instance, the human body can be compared to the church. Marriage is a symbol of the union between Christ and His church. Babies are born naked and crying, which symbolizes their sinful state. There is an emblem in green twigs that can be used to teach us about raising children. Flexible twigs signify young children because they can be easily trained and guided.

FRUIT TREE: Also, ripened fruit falls from our branches - gravity is a sign of God's love, for it keeps the universe in balance and creates a sense of beauty, harmony and order. And since the institution of marriage is a representation of the union between Christ and the Church, there are certainly many more things in the world that point to spiritual realities. Gravity and marriage serve as reminders of the divine love that keeps us all connected.

GRANDDAD: Temptation and sin are universal human experiences that are symbolized in everyday life. For example, when hunting, fishing, or trapping, bait is used to lure the prey. This is a representation of how the enemy uses our weaknesses and addictions to lead us into trouble. Similarly, dirt in the eyes can create a form of blindness that hinders our sight. This is symbolic of how the world can blind us if we focus too much on it. The crocodile is a representation of sin and temptation, as it is easier to defeat in the beginning and grows continually. It starts as a small egg and grows into a monster, growing as long as it lives. The serpent's tongue is a representation of the terrible power of the human tongue. Our teeth act as a barrier to keep our tongue in check. The world is full of temptation and immorality, as there is dirt and filth everywhere. A dead body is a representation of spiritual death, and sleep is a state of spiritual unpreparedness. The twists and turns of the intestines symbolize the labyrinth of the heart, and still waters represent deception and unhappiness. Lightning is associated with high things, such as steeples and towers, and this serves as a reminder that God will strike down those who are prideful. People of influence and authority need to have strong foundations to prevent them from toppling. Therefore, it is essential to be aware of the temptations and sin around us and to recognize the need for God's intervention and help.

FRUIT TREE: Many times I have seen predators, such as spiders and snakes, that often hide in dark, secret places and strike without warning!

GRANDDAD: The life of a believer is fraught with challenges and dangers - yet being called and born again to being sanctified and perfected is an adventure filled with emblematic treasures. Peter's repentance when he heard the cock crow symbolizes the proclamation of the Gospel. Roosters are a divine representation of preaching that jolts people from their guilty sleep. The wheat sown before winter symbolizes renewal in the life of a believer. It grows before winter and then appears to die as the cold sets in. It remains dormant until spring, when it wakes up and flourishes until it produces fruit. This is an emblem for the spiritual decline that many believers experience after conversion. They become lifeless, only to rise again and live a glorious Christian life. This image applies to both the church and the individual.

FRUIT TREE: Then we may infer from this, with our fruit tree wisdom, that revival often happens quickly after God prunes the church, just like blooms and new life come after the pruning of a fruit tree.

GRANDDAD: You are correct! In a similar way, true faith and grace are like a person waking up from a deep sleep. Another emblem is that of water not being able to rise higher than its source, illustrating humanity's inability to accomplish redemption apart from God's work. Just as there are many counterfeits of gold and diamonds, there are many false forms of religion. When the Spirit of the Lord is absent, evil is able to take over, and many people who initially profess faith in Christ end up abandoning it. The moon is a symbol of the elect, reflecting God's light and illuminating the darkness.

FRUIT TREE: May I also add that hypocrites are like dead wood on the ground. They may sprout in the springtime, but when the summer sun shines down, they quickly wither away, having no real root. The many blossoms that don't produce fruit on a tree are like the majority of people who make a show of faith in Christ but eventually turn away.

GRANDDAD: Your tree wisdom is very insightful!

———

GRANDDAD: The pains of childbirth represent the struggles of the church as it works to bring new life to believers, as well as the challenges an individual faces as Christ is formed in them. This new life is powered by a spiritual heart that constantly pumps for spiritual growth. Just like the formation of a baby in the womb, the spiritual life of a believer is dependent on the nourishment of God and the Holy Spirit.

FRUIT TREE: Believers are like fledgling birds, perched in the nest, mouths wide open, eagerly awaiting the nourishment of the Spirit. When God visits the church, believers should be ready to receive His blessings and be open to the revival and awakening that He brings.

GRANDDAD: Climbing a mountain or hill can be a challenging journey that takes a lot of hard work and dedication. It's much easier to go down than it is to go up, and it takes a lot of self-discipline to make it to the top. The view from the top is worth the effort, though, and it's a great reward for all the hard work. Similarly, a Christian life is full of difficult times and hard work, but the benefits of holiness and closeness to God are worth it. The opposite of this is hypocrites and backsliders, who give up and retreat down the mountain.

GRANDDAD: The Christian life is also like a garden that needs to be weeded periodically; the best time to do this is when it has rained, because then the ground is softer and it's easier to pull out the weeds without damaging the plants. Just like how a garden needs to be weeded, the church needs to be purified and disciplined, and this can only be done when there is a revival of religion. Adversity and trials are part of the Christian life, and they are like a refining process that purifies us and prepares us for service. It's like winter before spring; you have to go through the cold and the darkness before you can experience the warmth and the light. Pain and persecution are necessary steps to reach the desired outcome, just like metals need to be heated up and wheat needs to be winnowed. Suffering shapes us into the likeness of Christ, and it's all worth it in the end.

FRUIT TREE: The fair blossoms that fall from a fruit tree show the same downward tendency as those reluctant to climb mountains. Pretenders seem to show much promise, but ultimately produce nothing. They are like noisy streams of water during a rain shower that seem to go on forever but soon vanish when the rain is gone.

———

GRANDDAD: Contrary to adversity, during times of prosperity it's easy to become complacent and neglectful of our spiritual life. Prosperity and ease is like an endless summer, where pests and plagues can multiply without restraint. In order to achieve spiritual sanctification, we must experience times of humility and suffering, similar to the winter season. Just as plants wither without sunlight, so too can excessive light and comfort lead to pride and arrogance. The image of a falling object illustrates this concept. The higher the object is before it falls, the deeper the hole it makes. Similarly, those who have been raised to a higher place in knowledge, wealth, and religious privileges, will experience an often fatal fall if they become backsliders and hypocrites. An architectural analogy illustrates that before we can reach the mountaintop of spiritual exaltation, we must first descend into the valley of humiliation - much like a caterpillar precedes a butterfly.

GRANDDAD: Sanctification is similar to a child growing up. It doesn't happen all at once, but rather gradually over time. This is similar to how a believer's spiritual growth occurs. As we mature, we face obstacles and hardships, but instead of being loud and erratic like a shallow stream, we become deep like a river and are able to flow over them without making a sound.

FRUIT TREE: Similarly, young fruit starts off green and unripe, but as it is exposed to the warmth of the sun, it matures and reaches its peak, so too does a believer. Their new heart, which is filled with the Spirit of God, continues to beat until they are made perfect in holiness.

———

GRANDDAD: The sun and moon are emblems of Christ and the church, respectively. Just like a tree growing from a seed to a sprout and then to maturity, the church also goes through several different stages. Grains such as wheat and corn can be seen as a metaphor for the church. Food processing and cooking can be seen as a symbol of God's purification of his chosen people, preparing them for himself. God created man with the power to love a woman so deeply that it mirrors Christ's love for the church. If the woman that the man loves turns to someone else, it can cause extreme jealousy, similar to Christ's love for his bride, the church.

FRUIT TREE: As was mentioned earlier, a garden is a representation of the church as it is best to get rid of weeds after a rain shower to make it easier. When the Holy Spirit is poured out in revival, preaching of difficult doctrines and church discipline become easier.

———

GRANDDAD: The invention of telescopes which allows us to see the heavens more clearly is a sign of the immense progress in knowledge of the heavens in the end times.

FRUIT TREE: Telescopes sound similar to the "spectacles of faith" through which we are now viewing the world.

GRANDDAD: Indeed, the two are related. This vision can sometimes cause tears of sadness which symbolize the sorrow experienced by those who see God (Isaiah 6:1, 5; Luke 5:8).

GRANDDAD: Also, as a fruit tree you certainly understand that the transition from winter to summer corresponds to the gradual growth of the church. A sudden change would be catastrophic.

FRUIT TREE: We know that all too well.

———

GRANDDAD: Grand assemblies, parades, and coronations on earth are foreshadows of the Judgment Day in Heaven, where both the righteous and the wicked will be judged.

GRANDDAD: Concerning the last things, physical death brings with it pain and suffering, but those in Christ can experience victory over death and receive life everlasting. The transformation of the silkworm into a butterfly is symbolic of the resurrection of believers. For those who do not follow God, death is a punishment, like a pig to the slaughter. The end of worldly men is likened to a bubble, expanding and shimmering with vibrant colors before bursting and disappearing. For the saint, death is like a ripe fruit falling from the tree, ready to leave this world for Heaven. The kernel of corn, the rising sun, and waking up from a deep sleep are all symbols of resurrection. The sun's never-ending radiance and the river's continual flowing into the ocean are symbols of eternity. Trees by a river represent the saints' never-ending source of the Holy Spirit, while a buried body with no power to rise is an emblem of hell's everlasting misery.

GRANDDAD: The death of insects, fighting spiders in jars, and other creatures that are not ready for what's to come, symbolize the suffering and judgment that will befall the wicked and those who don't believe in God. When a notorious criminal is put on trial and sentenced, a large group of important people will be there to witness it. This is just a small example of the great and final judgment, in which sinners will be officially condemned to everlasting punishment. It will be a glorious day, like the sun rising in the sky. The Son of God will shine His light and banish the darkness, sending Satan to the depths of the abyss.

————

GRANDDAD: On a peaceful day, the majestic beauty of the sky reflects the calmness of those who have made it to heaven. The vastness of the heavens is a reminder of the great difference between the magnificence of the sky and that of the earth. Mountains signify heaven and the difficulty of getting there. Just like how one must go through low points to reach the peak of a mountain, one must go through hardship to reach the highest point of heaven. The higher you climb, the smaller and more insignificant the things below become. As mountain climbers reach the summit, they experience a sense of tranquility. Those who make it to heaven will be in a state of absolute bliss forever. Birds soaring in the sky symbolize the saints in heaven. The never-ending blue of the sky is a representation of the eternal glory of heaven. The stars that twinkle from generation to generation demonstrate the everlasting beauty of heaven.

FRUIT TREE: Also, when a fruit is ripe, it easily falls from the tree. Likewise, when a person is prepared for the heaven, they effortlessly leave this life.

GRANDDAD: True! Nothing on earth can compare to the joy of heaven. When viewed from space, the world's tallest mountains and valleys look small. This illustrates how the wealth and honor of the world will look insignificant when seen from a heavenly perspective. The grandeur of this world is nothing compared to the eternal blessings of heaven. The sky is much higher than the highest point on earth, signifying the immense joy of heaven compared to the happiness of this world. Even the most influential people in this world cannot find true happiness. Just like how one could be a free citizen of Rome and enjoy its privileges even when living far away, one can be a citizen of heaven and bask in its glory even from afar. The only way to find true satisfaction is in heaven.

FRUIT TREE: The thorns of a rose bush represent the trials and difficulties that come with life. The rose is the last to blossom, symbolizing the ultimate reward for perseverance.

GRANDDAD: This is wisdom.

———

GRANDDAD: The eternal alternative is terrifying. The tormenting nature of hell is symbolized by worms devouring a rotting corpse, a stark contrast to the heavenly splendors. Hell's inhabitants are as repulsive as the corpse, and the Flood of Noah's day is similar to the destruction and lake of fire that is hell. Volcanic eruptions that pour liquid fire on cities represent God's retribution, and spiders confined together symbolize the devil's destructive nature. Animals shrieking and wailing in the night represent the agonizing cries of the people in hell.

FRUIT TREE: The emblems of heaven and hell are wonderful and terrifying. As I consider your reflections on the Bible and the world around us, I'm overwhelmed by the complexity and depth of it all. It's impossible to fully comprehend the magnitude of what we can learn from these two sources of revelation!

The Awakening

THE DIALOG BETWEEN MY GRANDDAD and the fruit tree becomes increasingly quiet, and I find myself slipping away from the orchard. Suddenly, I'm sitting on a bed, looking out the window at the wonderful sight of a pure blue sky above fields of lush green grass, with a lone tree on the horizon. My body and thoughts are filled with the conversation between my granddad and the fruit tree. I can feel it. It's a sensation I've never had before. I'm exhausted, and my body begins to relax. I'm in the perfect spot of tranquility.

I wake up and hear a gentle, rolling thunder and feel drops of rain on my face. I had a dream, but was it a dream? My entire being feels changed. Everything seems more vivid and real. The rain starts to fall harder. When I glance at the box of books, I know they're about to become wet, so I quickly close the lid and dash towards the house. I'm too exhausted to go upstairs to the attic, so I sit in my granddad's study, trying to process what I've experienced. Physically, I am fatigued.

Granddad enters the study after hearing me come it. He notices that I am a little excited.

"Are you okay?" he asks.

"I was out in the orchard, and I fell asleep while reading some of your books," I explain. "I dreamed about you!"

"Really? Tell me about it,"

"You were talking with the trees," I say quietly.

"Oh, I see..."

Then everything comes out. I begin telling him about my dream, or what I recall of it. It's all a little blurry and out of focus, but not so much that I can't remember the essence of it. It is, in fact, the longest and most vivid dream I have ever had. I may have only slept for a half-hour in the orchard, but the dream seemed to go on for several days.

Granddad is staring at me, not saying anything. He begins to talk after I finish explaining the entire experience, then pauses.

"What you've told me is fascinating. Normally, I would point you to a Bible verse or tell you not to overthink your dreams. However, what you experienced is extraordinary, and I believe it has great theological significance."

"Have you ever heard of Victor Hugo?" he inquires.

I shake my head and say, "No."

He goes to a shelf and takes a book from there, then he turns to a marked page.

"In his novel, *Les Misérables,* he writes, 'Animals are merely forms of our virtues and vices, wandering before our eyes, the visible phantoms of our souls. God shows them to us to make us reflect... they are merely shadows...'"

Granddad continues reading, "Hugo observes Inspector Javert's wolf-like qualities and explains why his outward demeanor is a true reflection of his inward character: 'It is our conviction that if souls were visible to the eye we would see clearly the strange fact that each individual of the human species corresponds to some species of the animal kingdom; and we would easily recognize the truth, scarcely perceived by thinkers, that from the oyster to the eagle, from the pig to the tiger, all animals are in man, and that each of them is in each man; sometimes even several of them at a time... The peasants of the Asturias believe that in every litter of wolves there is one pup that is killed by the mother for fear that on growing up it would devour the other little ones. Give a human face to this wolf's son and you will have Javert.'"

He pauses, then closes the book.

"Davy," he says, "vivid comparisons, metaphors, and correspondences are characteristics of great writing that are widely accepted and expected in the literary world. Victor Hugo's Javert, with his wolf-like features, is similar to Jonathan Edwards' deep emblematic theology, which you have been reading. Edwards observed that people and animals share many parallels, recalling Jesus' words in Matthew 10:16, 'Behold, I am sending you out as sheep among wolves, so be wise as serpents and innocent as doves.'"

"God created the world for us to reflect on and contemplate in order for Him to teach us spiritual things. He frequently teaches us through allegories, parables, and types, encouraging us to exercise and grow in our understanding of divine things. God created the universe in such a way that it rhymes with and reinforces the teaching of the Bible."

Granddad says many of the same things he said in the dream.

The phone suddenly rings, and Granddad answers it, probably to speak with someone from the church. I leave the study and return to the living room, where I gaze out the window. I have so much to think about that it nearly seems overwhelming. My entire world has been turned upside down in the last 30 minutes or so. I can't shake the feeling, but it's not anxiousness that I feel; that has gone away. It has been replaced by a sense of amazement and expectancy. I gaze out the window at the distant orchard.

The wind is blowing through the trees, and the leaves are rustling. The sky is still cloudy, yet it appears tranquil. Thunderstorms and lightning are no longer frightening. I can see in the distance the green area of grass beneath the tree where I napped.

Everything appears to be more perfect, beautiful, and peaceful. There is hope, beauty, and an overall sense of purpose and meaning. My unease, isolation, and sense of loss are starting to fade. When I return my gaze to the orchard, I notice a shaft of light breaking through the clouds. Hope. Then I notice something else when I look down the driveway, I see a girl carrying a basket, followed by a small puppy. Suze has arrived to gather apples. That was the reason for the phone call. I dash out the front door to greet her. I'll go apple picking with her and tell her about the dream. I have a feeling she'll understand.

Thunder God, Wonder God:
Exploring the Emblematic Vision of Jonathan Edwards

Robert L. Boss (Jonathan Edwards Society Press, 2023)

(Hardcover 978-1737902676, Paperback 978-1737902652)

"Although scholars have long known about Jonathan Edwards' fascination with signs, symbols, types, and emblems, Robert Boss's study goes well beyond what others have done before. His wide-ranging comparison of Edwards with other figures of the period, but especially his exhaustive catalog of images ("emblems") in nature from which Edwards drew deep spiritual meaning, adds significantly to understanding Edwards. The book also suggests how Edwards' use of emblems could aid contemporary believers in finding more riches in Scripture as well as seeing more of Providence in the natural world."

> **Mark A. Noll**, author of *The Rise of Evangelicalism:*
> *The Age of Edwards, Whitefield, and the Wesleys*

"Rob Boss has done it again. This is a marvelous introduction to Edwards' typological vision. Enchanting indeed."

> **Douglas A. Sweeney**, Beeson Divinity School
> Samford University

"This is a deeply fascinating book which demonstrates how out of touch we moderns are with Edwards's God-centered vision of the world. Boss takes us deep into Edwards's typological and emblematic interpretation of nature, giving us both a rich scholarly study as well as a 'how to' manual packed with visuals designed to stir our theological imagination in Edwardsean ways. Many thanks to Rob Boss for pointing us back to Edwards's God-infused vision of interpreting the natural world!"

> **Robert W. Caldwell III**, Professor of Church History
> Southwestern Baptist Theological Seminary